TWENTY GRAND

TWENTY GRAND

And Other Tales of Love and Money

REBECCA CURTIS

HARPER ⬤ PERENNIAL

NEW YORK • LONDON • TORONTO • SYDNEY

HARPER ● PERENNIAL

Grateful acknowledgment is made to the venues in which the following
were published: "Hungry Self," "The Alpine Slide," and "Twenty Grand"
in *The New Yorker*; "The Alpine Slide" also appeared in *Harper's Bazaar*'s
Big Red Book (2006); "Twenty Grand" also appeared in *Harper's Goddess*
(2007); "Summer, with Twins" and "Big Bear, California" in *Harper's*
magazine; "To the Interstate" in *Conjunctions*; "The Near-Son" in *n+1*;
"Monsters" in *Crowd*; "Knick, Knack, Paddywhack" in *Fence*; "The Wolf at
the Door" in *StoryQuarterly*; and "Solicitation" and "The Sno-Kone Cart"
in *McSweeney's*.

P.S.™ is a trademark of HarperCollins Publishers.

HarperCollins books may be purchased for educational, business, or sales
promotional use. For information please write: Special Markets Depart-
ment, HarperCollins Publishers, 10 East 53rd Street, New York, NY 10022.

FIRST EDITION

Designed by Justin Dodd

Library of Congress Cataloging-in-Publication Data is available upon request.

ISBN: 978-0-06-117309-7
ISBN-10: 0-06-117309-6

07 08 09 10 11 ID/RRD 10 9 8 7 6 5 4 3 2 1

CONTENTS

HUNGRY SELF

THE STARS WERE BEGINNING above the lake, and the boats with their tiny pilot lights were entering the bay through the channel to dock for the night. Johnny, Ngoc's son, was lighting the red evening candles with half an eye on me, because he liked to keep an eye on the help, or maybe because his mother had taught him to. I had a layer of oil on my face. My apron was shiny with duck sauce, and my pockets were puffy with crumpled dollar bills. We'd had Buffet Day earlier. On Buffet Day we got a lot of families and fat people who came because the other people who came were fat and no one was too embarrassed to load up a really tall plate, and people stayed a few hours to double-eat and left bunches of ones for tips.

I was watching Johnny glide across the dark-red carpet, menus in hand, to seat someone at the last booth in the lakeside row. Like me, he was watching the boats. I was terribly in love with him, but we were separated by race and by the fact that he hated me. Johnny was nineteen, which was my age, and we had both spent every night of the summer here—I did it because I was broke and Johnny did it because Ngoc was a widow and needed him to help her run this restaurant she'd maintained after her husband's death so that Johnny could maintain it after her own. He lit the little red candle in the booth, where he'd seated a lonely and enormous woman, and nodded at me on his way to the kitchen. I went over to the table and put down some dry noodles and a stained silver teapot and turned over a white china cup and poured some tea in it, and the woman swiveled her body toward mine and gave me the smile you give a waitress if you're the kind of person who is nice to a waitress, and I saw that the woman was my ex-psychiatrist. I knocked over the cup and the tea spilled onto the table and then onto her lap.

I'm sorry, I said, I'm sorry.

I watched her face go through a set of, "If A, then B; if B, then C; A, therefore C," after which she said, Hi, how are you?, as if to say, Is everything OK, now? with an element of I am neither your mother nor your relative but I do care for you to the extent that my highly stretched human resources allow, and I said, Good, good, to mean Everything is good, your efforts were successful, and please feel happy about the energy you invested in me.

The next day was the start of Bike Week, a five-day festival during which a hundred thousand bikers would arrive and celebrate being bikers in our very small and very beautiful town. On the last night of that week, I would have fourteen tables and I would tell them their food was almost ready but that would be a lie, since I'd mismatched three tables' worth of orders and none of them would eat sooner than an hour after being sat, and they would each tip me nothing, to say You are worth nothing, or one dollar, to say You are worth crap; except for those people who were nicest and least likely to complain and whom I would therefore serve last. They would not eat for an hour and a half. These people would tip me a twenty and I would wonder at their foolishness and give the twenty to Ken the cook, who sold coke in the basement, and who'd been shipped in by Ngoc from China and housed in a rat-shack next door. He knew how to say "shitfucker" and "asslick" and had a habit of wiping his dick with his hands then not washing them after and telling me about it, charades style.

Ngoc knew about this but couldn't do much. She was old and strange-looking and dyed her hair black and wore rhinestone-studded mauve gowns that she thought added elegance to the general atmosphere of the restaurant. The restaurant was very red and very gold. Ngoc bussed tables and supervised the kitchen, and the bar, and us, and at night I watched her bending over the counter in front, adding columns of figures without a calculator. She couldn't control the cooks, but she kept them on because they were illegal and worked cheap. All of the cooks were wrinkled and small and had perms; once a month, they pitched in and took a cab downtown, where they bought hookers and sat for their perms.

Ken the cook cut five wide lines for a twenty in a boxed-goods room behind the meat rack in the basement, which is where Ngoc would find us, and Ngoc would be in an intolerant mood that night because the same bikers who came every year, a group of them, fat and bearded and staggering drunk, had stopped her in the lobby and chanted, Ngoc, Ngoc, Ngoc, give us a chink hug Ngoc, give us a chink hug, and Ngoc had had to totter on over in her heels and her Elvira dress and scream, So good to see you! So good to see you! and press herself against each one of their enormous bodies. When Ngoc found the cook and me doing lines in the basement she'd have some things to say to us in Cantonese and then some things to say to us in English, which would be that there is one kind of trash and there is another kind of trash and neither kind was trash that she wanted in her Eating Establishment.

But this shift was slow. I'd spent most of it putting purple tissue umbrellas in drinks and asking customers what they'd seen in town so far and telling them where they might want to go. And, even though they did not want and had not ordered dessert, I'd been bringing out ten fortune cookies on an egg-roll plate with a pile of pineapple chunks topped by whipped cream and my specialty, umbrella-lodged-in-cherry, because I remembered, when I was kid, how excited I'd been whenever we went out to eat Chinese and how, despite the fact that we took ten minutes to study the menu, we always knew exactly what we would order, which was pork fried rice, sweet n sour chicken, egg fu yung, and beef teriyaki, none of which were really Chinese, and I remembered how the waitress would bring out, for the finale, a plate heaped with cherries and pineapple chunks, and once my sister's cookie had said, "You will discover great wealth," and then in the parking lot she found a dime and for years after that I waited for my cookies to come true.

The cherries and umbrellas came from Jud the bartender and Jud did not like my taking them, but he let me because he was short and missing two teeth and wanted to fuck me. He had a boat and a house on the promenade and was one of those people who sat on their widow's walk on bright days and watched the tourists, evaluating their stupidity or level of ugliness. I'm going boating this week, he'd say. Want to go boating? Next week, I'd say, and he'd say, Remind me. He looked a little like James Dean, some people had told him, and this is what kept him happy, I think.

IN THE KITCHEN I found towels to clean up the tea. My ex-psychiatrist was my ex-counselor, really, ex–family counselor, one in a long line of psychiatrists that at first my family, and then just I, had consulted. She was a fat ugly lesbian. Her partner, or maybe just her lover, had arrived while I was fetching the towels. I say "lover" because they seemed to be on a date. They were nervous with happiness and had elected to sit next to each other, on the same side of the booth, facing one of the restaurant's decorative highlights, a red and gold dragon gleefully humping a column. I figured this side-by-side seating arrangement to be an announcement of love, a fuck-you to the world, and I was embarrassed for them, and for myself, to be serving my ex-psychiatrist, here, in this shitty place, and for her to be eating here, in this shitty place, because she weighed two hundred and sixty pounds and there was nothing on our menu that it was a good idea for her to eat. She'd never told me what she weighed but I knew anyway because I was an excellent evaluator of bodily weight; this ability was, in part, why three years ago I had driven weekly to her horrible office.

I was standing with my waitress notepad at my chest. The boats were sliding into their places at the docks. Johnny was looking on from the lobby, to make sure I did not spill any more tea, and I thought about pleading stomachache so I could leave early and not have to serve dinner to my ex-shrink, but that would have sounded as if I had my period, which would have been gross, and Johnny liked me little enough already.

My ex-psychiatrist said, This is my friend Angela. Then we had a round of inquiry and solicitation, which was not strictly necessary since we would probably not see each other again. This woman had sat across from me for six months and had told me repeatedly that I was not a bad person, was in fact a good person, and because I do not like to talk and managed to get her to talk instead, she told me that people had been unkind to her all her life and that she had suffered great sadness and once tried to end it all with some cooking oil and a match, but ended up instead with a fist-sized patch of blackness on her skull and soft white skin grafts on her calves, and that she was now dealing with an eating disorder herself, which was obesity, and that she found that Harry's Diet Pretzels were a wonderful help and made you feel full and at peace, as if you did not need anything else, and she gave me an extra bag that she happened to have in her purse because the sadness could come upon you at any time, and it was best to have Harry's Diet Pretzels with you when it did.

I took their orders. I recommended lo mein. I said, Everyone likes it. I did not say, Everyone likes it because it is noodles in oil and you will like it too. They ordered lo mein and Szechuan grand worbar, a fancy chicken thing that sizzles over a blue flame on an iron plate in front of the customer, which I normally liked to serve because it guaranteed a good tip. I did not want a good tip. I wanted a shitty tip. I wanted a shitty tip so I could have a reason for hating the fat ugly lesbian, a reason other than that she had once seen me cry.

The lover was polite in a cold, challenging way. I said Ngoc's special tea was shipped straight from Shanghai and that our cook was famous in Hong Kong, and she nodded as if something unpleasant had just been confirmed. I guessed how their pre-soup conversation would go:

Former patient?

Yes.

Bad one?

Yes.

Think she's better now?

Probably not. I hope so. She means well.

I DELIVERED a pineapple plate to a family of seven who had ordered cheap and were excited to see it. Johnny was waiting for me in the kitchen, leaning against the industrial tea bins.

You know those women?

I had a tray full of chicken bones and half-eaten egg fu yung from the happy family. I set my tray on the wash counter and removed the plates and started slopping them off and immediately got some of the slop on my shirt.

You know them? he repeated.

Nope.

What'd they order? Lo mein?

Yup.

He took the tray from me and stashed it with the other trays.

Last party. You're off for the night.

Great. I kept slopping.

You going out?

I racked my dishes and wiped myself.

I don't know.

You got some gravy on your shirt.

I wiped myself again.

Let me know if there's anything going on.

Sure, I said. There was not anything going on, but I wondered what constituted Going On and how I could spin a night of nothing going on into Something Going On, and if he would like that, and if he did like that, if he'd like me. But I knew that he did not like me. He was a color in the sea of white that was this state, and he seldom spoke and had no friends, although he worked out all the time and was beautiful. When he mowed the littered and weedy lawn that sloped from the restaurant down to the lake, the other waitresses and I found reasons to walk by the open windows every ten minutes or so. Once, at the end of a day when Ngoc had been ill and Johnny had spent twelve hours ferrying unsatisfied customers in and out of the enormous red dining room, I found him sitting in the waitress station in front of a pile of pink drink umbrellas he'd ruined by pushing them open too forcefully. He'd said, I hate this, meaning this place, and I could tell he hated us, the staff, just as Ngoc hated us, and I guessed Ngoc would import a wife for him as she had for his retarded brother, who was twenty-nine and watched cartoons in the lobby and told knock-knock jokes and did not know how to fuck his wife and actually liked us.

I went downstairs to the basement. It was vast and unlit and I liked it, because down there I was just a person in the basement of a Chinese restaurant. I made my way around the meat racks, which were the size of twin beds and held whole bloody sides of beef. Between dark isles of boxed goods there were gallon cans of sweet and sour and plastic bags of dry noodles, and one aisle was full of weird figurines—Buddhas and dull golden phoenixes. Ken the cook was sitting there, in the dark, on a cardboard box, hands limp in his lap.

Hi, honey, he said. When he smiled, his mouth was a black pit with white spots. I pulled the chain of the lightbulb.

Shitfuck! he screamed.

I pulled the chain again. I didn't really need light.

Hey, he said.

What, I said.

He pointed at the box where he'd set up the lines. You every ten minute. Kill yourself. Stupid. Then he started talking again, but this time he wasn't talking to me and I didn't understand what he was saying anyway. I went ahead, but took less than my share, to prove I wasn't stupid.

I BROUGHT my ex-psychiatrist and her lover their soup. It was egg drop, the soup most likely to have a roach at the bottom. All the soups were left in uncovered vats on a table in the kitchen overnight, but egg drop is thick and yellow and made primarily of yolk, so that the roaches remain undetected at the bottom of the cup until the bulk of the soup has been eaten. I should add that this wasn't Ngoc's fault. Once a month Ngoc made us move all the cups and plates into the dining room, and the exterminators would arrive with their hoses and spray and then we'd put the stuff back, but it never made a difference. You could pick up a platter or a pile of napkins or a cookie and there'd be a roach underneath.

When their soup came back, the cups looked O.K.: no roaches. My ex-psychiatrist and her lover were happy. They were holding hands. Apparently, my ex-psychiatrist was right-handed and her lover was left-handed and they could hold hands and eat at the same time. When I brought their dinner plates, my ex-psychiatrist asked me, Was I at school and did I like it, meaning, was I better? I would take a year off school that fall and move in with an ex-attorney who was dealing some to finance his business-school tuition, and my one year off would stretch into five; but I did not know that yet and I said, Yes, I was at school, and I like it.

In the kitchen, Ken asked did I want to lick his cock, which was one of the things he knew how to say, and I said, Lao Shi, which I thought meant "Asshole" but which I later learned meant "Teacher." My other tables had finished their dinners. I was nearly done for the night. I stood in the kitchen hoping Johnny might come in, because I felt I was ready to tell him there was something going on. Ngoc and her retarded son and the cooks were playing mah-jongg on the floor. Ngoc had lit the kitchen shrine—a candle in front of a foot-high Buddha with three oranges at its base. She had a glass of something from the bar and was screeching and laughing periodically, which seemed to indicate that she was lessening her vigilance, but when she saw me standing and waiting for Johnny she said I could polish pupu platters or fold napkins if I wasn't busy, so I ducked back into the dining room.

In the dark, the lit globes on the tables looked elegant. Outside, the pilot lights of the boats were still moving slowly through the channel. At midnight, there would be fireworks you could watch from the water or the beach. This happened every Friday night; it was part of the town's effort to make itself attractive to vacationers and perhaps to itself. I was living on a nearby island with two girls, twins, whose parents had money and let them live in a house on this island that was connected to the mainland by a bridge. When these girls finished college they would decide not to be investment bankers after all but to move to Venice Beach instead to try to break into movies, and then television, and then commercials. I'm still waiting to see them in commercials. I would like for something to happen for these girls, particularly because that night I decided people should come over to the house, lots of people, and I would in fact begin inviting people at the restaurant and continue doing so all the way home, walking along the boulevard in my skirt, so that there would be something going on to bring Johnny to, and this party would end in a fire that would climb from a guest bedroom to the attic and the roof, and which would make this the last summer these girls spent on this island.

I set up my prep tray by the lesbians' table so that when their food was ready they could see their Szechuan grand worbar flame up in front of them. This woman, my former psychiatrist, or former family counselor, and her partner, or lover, were talking so intently, about something so deeply philosophical (I gathered from the few words I caught) that I felt a certain sadness. She no longer pretended to be obliged to talk to me, as if she knew it was a larger kindness to simply let me be her waitress and not someone she had once known.

The first time we met, my entire family had driven out to her home. There was a "Welcome Friends" wreath on the door and decorative wooden ducks in the hall. We sat in her living room and my father made her cry. She asked some questions, which I answered, and my father said some things that were not answers to the questions, and she told him to please refrain from interrupting others or speaking in a loud, angry tone, and he said she really knew nothing about our family, since she was not part of our family, and that she in fact had interrupted him, and that so far her ideas were crazy, and that in his family, since he was the father, he would speak when he wanted to speak and say what he wanted to say.

My mother had nodded and put a hand on his leg and said his name in the tone of voice in which someone says, Stop, but which really meant, "I am your partner in life and I love you whatever you do," because when she spoke she told the lesbian, We need you to work with us. You are not working with us. Then the lesbian said that perhaps it was a good idea for each of my parents, my father particularly, to come individually for counseling, as there seemed to be some issues all around that might bear discussion, and then my father had some things to say about this house we were in and this lesbian counselor and what he thought of her effectiveness, her intelligence, and her persona, and then the lesbian took a time-out break.

We sat in silence and heard her blubber in the bathroom. It was the happiest time we had known. My mother's hand was on my father's knee. I might have been smirking a little, I don't know why, except that in times of great tension or truth-telling I smirk; also I was pleased to see my father's attention directed at someone else for an extended duration of time.

After that first appointment, at the lesbian's insistence, I was told to go with either my mother or my father, not both, to her office, not her home. But that only happened once, because my father made her cry again. During our second visit, he called her a Monstrous Fat Pig. I'd found a book about menopause on her office shelf and was reading it because I was pleased that my father and the lesbian had found plenty to talk about by themselves, when my father said, You must weigh . . .

He turned to me. What does she weigh?

Two-sixty, I said.

Two-sixty, he said. You weigh two-sixty and you think you can tell me what to do, how to discipline my own daughter, how to talk to my own daughter? The lesbian counselor cried pretty soon after that. There might have been more words on my father's part—"manipulative," maybe "controlling," "disappointing," and "freakish aberration of nature." These were words that we both liked. We drove home in a happy silence, almost a camaraderie, in which he said, Beautiful day, and How is school, and How is track—a mood which would last approximately until midnight, when I would puke in the kitchen sink and he would walk downstairs from where he had not been sleeping and tell me that I was a shitty little mess who was destroying the family, which was his family, and had I not considered taking myself away to somewhere not this house, because if I did not he surely would take himself away, and how did I imagine my brothers and my mother would feel about that?

MY ORDER was up. I got the chicken worbar into its vat and trucked the hot iron plate out and set it down on the prep tray and produced a Sterno can from my pocket. I held the match high for drama before I lit it, and when the Sterno caught the two women clapped. Then I put the can on the plate and poured the chicken from the vat onto the plate, being careful not to pour any into the can itself.

If there's anything else I can do, I said, let me know. Then I went to fold napkins. I did this at a hidden station in the corner of the dining room. I was secretly watching them. They were talking about something I'm sure they did not give a shit about, but they clearly liked each other, and not in a sex way or a passing way but with some deep and generous mutual admiration, enough that they assumed, if they saw me at all, that I was only folding napkins, or watching the bow lights of the boats jostling for dock space at the pier, and not watching them, waiting for them to be done.

Johnny came over and sat with me. I kept folding.

Hey, he said.

Hey, I said.

He took a pile and folded.

I think there's something going on, I said. I told him the people I lived with were having a party. I said Jud would be there. I said other people that he knew would be there. I said he should come. I said that I, in particular, hoped he would come.

He said he had a few other things going on. Then he said maybe he'd come. He paused. Then he said he'd come when he got off work. I got up and left the table because I didn't know what to say next.

The lesbians were looking at me the way you look at a waitress when you're too content to crook your finger at her. I went over to their table. They said they would like, if it was not too much trouble, to take their food home in a box. I tried not to think, while I packed the box, that they would be better off without the extra food, or wonder whether they would eat it that night, individually or together, or how many hours would pass before the sadness would come back.

It was after my father called my shrink a pig that I began going to see her alone and that she suggested the special pretzels. For twenty weeks this counselor woman saw me at half rate, because my parents would not pay more, and listened to me talk about school or books or people I liked or did not like and what I wished I had done at a certain time or what I wished I had not done, and handed me tissues when she finally got me to cry, and told me that I was a good person, a smart person, a person with whom she liked to talk, and I said, Thank you, thank you, at the end of each hour, and she said, Hug me, and I did, and once she gave me a book, which I was supposed to return by mail but never did, which was pink and called *Healing the Hungry Self* and had careful marginalia at important places in her handwriting, where I wrote, What a fat pig, go on a diet, fat pig, a book I read three times in the hope of being cured.

THAT NIGHT THE party would happen. In just a few hours many people would arrive on the island in many cars and carry many bottles of alcohol into the house, which would be lit up, every room, and bottles and lamps would get broken and someone would have brass knuckles and someone else would have a gun and it would get so that Johnny and I had to go outside, down to the beach, and sit on the sand and watch the sky, dizzy with light, and the water, candy-fish bright. There was an anchored dock floating about thirty feet out, and I fixed on the idea of our spending the night on our backs, not talking or touching, but silently being together, and I would open my backpack, there at the beach, the air was still enough, and take out the stash I'd borrowed off Ken and say, I like to do this sometimes, and he'd say, I don't think I want to do that, and I'd say, Don't then, and leave him a line, and he would say, Why not, and he would like it.

My ex-shrink and her lover were waiting. I brought them the super pineapple dish. I watched them spear pineapple. Ngoc was cursing in the kitchen because she was losing at mah-jongg and the cooks were taking her money again. I heard the resounding low note of a fry pan hitting a soup vat and then the thud of an industrial tea bin crashing against the tiles. The copper lights of the promenade were blinking above the water and a firework flared up prematurely and failed to ignite and the dust cloud spread out against the sky and fell across the waiting white boats.

My ex-psychiatrist came over and took my hand on her way out. I was still folding napkins.

It was so good to see you, she said.

It was good to see you too, I said. But I didn't mean it.

Their table was neat, almost pre-cleaned, as if they had foreseen the work I would have to do and wanted to help. The little umbrellas, chopstick wrappers, and soiled napkins were piled on their plates and their chopsticks and silverware were neatly crossed. The tip was good, so as to say, We like you, but not too good, so as to say, We feel bad for you; obviously you are not cured; obviously, you've failed yourself and us. She'd left a cookie at the edge of the table and I took it and ate it. Then I saw the note she'd left, in familiar blue pen, on the check, as if I were someone she knew well or someone she still wanted to help. It said, You are kind-hearted, gentle, and beloved.

SUMMER, WITH TWINS

THAT SUMMER I LIVED with the Serrano twins in their parents' summerhouse. I'd met the twins at college, and even though the university was large, everyone knew them and just called them "the twins." There were other twins, like Hami and Hamid, two Iranian guys who smiled at, greeted, and bowed their heads to everyone they'd ever met as they walked across the campus, but none of them mattered. The twins were two girls, five foot eight, with long, straight brown hair that fell exactly halfway down their backs. They were athletic, high school soccer stars, with faces you'd never notice if there weren't two of them, oval and a little indignant-looking—they had full lips, dark brown eyes, and chins that jutted out when they talked. When I first met them, I wondered what all the fuss was about, because they seemed stupid. They got Cs in their economics classes, even though that was their major. They thought Singapore was a city in China, and once they'd spent an hour looking for Persia on a map. They weren't strikingly beautiful, and they weren't especially kind. But everything they did they did with enthusiasm: if they ate a bite of food, the food was delicious; if they kissed a boy, the kiss was long and deep; and if they went to sleep, the sleep was dreamless and divine. Their enthusiasm made me angry, because it seemed false, but then I became included in it and realized it was genuine.

After a few weeks, I'd learned to tell them apart: Jean's eyebrows were darker, thicker, and closer to her eyes, and Jessica's lips were larger and her cheeks were fat, a beautiful bedroom face, as if made as a place for a hand or another face to rest. She was three minutes younger, sweeter, quicker to anger, and quicker to forgive. Later, after our friendship ended, maybe their interests diverged, but when I knew them they took the same classes, spent all their time together, argued over their shared clothes, and, as far as politics, they were in agreement: they favored self-starters, a free economy, and zero government intervention.

Their father was a banker, and they planned to be bankers, too, and dropped financial phrases into everything they said.

The twins knew I needed money for college and had told me this town where their parents had a summerhouse was chock-full of expensive restaurants. We would all waitress at one of them, they said, and over the summer, make a killing. In high school the restaurant I'd bussed tables at served only sandwiches, so I said yes. I'd been surprised when the twins and I became friends, because in terms of the college, I didn't exist; but they thought I was funny. The first day we met, we went out to lunch. At lunch, they watched me squeeze my lemon into my water. Then they watched me open one pink fake sweetener and one blue one, pour them into the water, and stir the drink with my straw. Jessica asked to try a sip. She proclaimed it delicious. A minute later, Jean tried a sip. Her eyes went wide with delight.

It's poor man's lemonade! she said.

She squeezed her own lemon into her own water and added one blue sweetener and one pink. You're so funny! she said. I love it!

From then on, every time we went out to lunch we all drank poor man's lemonade. I had to come stay for the summer, they said, because they sometimes grew bored with each other, and they always got along better if someone else was around.

When I arrived, I was thrilled. The twins' parents' summerhouse wasn't the nicest one on the lake, but it was two stories, of white brick, and had a large back deck and a backyard that dropped down to a beach. The windows of the house let sun in all day long, the lake was deep and clear and had a sandy bottom, and in the garage was an ancient red Fiat the twins said could do 130 on the straightaways of the town.

THE RESTAURANT the twins had picked was the Christmas Inn, which was on the main route, by the waterfront. One long rectangular room in front was the dining room, and a narrow, rather trapezoidal space behind it was the bar. Both rooms had green shag rugs and a lot of green linen table-cloths. Despite the single, multitiered crystal chandelier and the marble façade in the foyer, it wasn't a prepossessing place. But it served seafood and steak, and the menu was overpriced. After filling out our applications, we met Boris, the owner and head cook, a man with a huge stomach and longish silver curls on his head. He had merry blue eyes, a bulbous mauve nose, and cracked pink lips. He was wearing a white T-shirt, tan shorts, and a bloody half-apron. His arms were thick, his posture erect, and his gut sailed before him like a flock of decapitated geese. He glanced at our applications, saw that we had no experience, and said they looked good. The restaurant, he said, could use pretty girls. Then he looked at the woman who was moving through the dining room, setting tables for dinner. She was maybe forty-five and had short black hair, olive skin, and droopy, off-kilter eyes.

Of course we have Dina, he said. We've had Dina for what, how long now, ten years?

The woman said something without turning around. Boris gave us a look. Then he called her over and told her to show us the kitchen.

Thanks for showing us everything, Jean said, when she was done.

Don't thank me, Dina said. I was doing my job.

Well, thank you anyway, Jean said.

Just what we need, Dina said. Three girls with no experience.

·　　·　　·

WHEN THE TWINS and I got home we went for an evening swim in the lake and then sat in the living room, eating buttered popcorn and watching TV.

We got a job, Jean said.

Dina's skanky, Jessica said.

Waitresses are like that when they're older, Jean said. It's from waitressing too long. They get a hardened, slutty look. She turned to me. Know what I mean?

I didn't really. But I wanted to seem like I did, so I nodded and said, You mean she looks like a wench.

What's a wench? Jean said.

It's like a hardened slut, I said.

Oh, Jean said. Then yeah. That's exactly what I meant.

WE WORKED FOR two weeks under Dina's tutelage. Each night, at Dina's direction, we brought Dina's tables their drinks, served her tables food, and cleared her tables' dirty dishes, then set the tables back up and handed her the tips. She would take the money, fold the bills, and put them in her apron. By the time our legs were numb, our bodies salty with sweat and our hair oiled with it, Dina would be dressed in her coat—thin, black, with a tattered fringe edge. She'd wait for us by the door. Then she'd thank us, say she was sorry it wasn't much, and give us each a few bucks.

What a wench, the twins said, on the way home, the first time it happened.

We're having our last fun summer, Jessica said. Her hair flapped over the front seat of the car, and jasmine strands struck my face. Beyond the road, enormous pines bowed toward one another and bulbous lamps glowed on granite blocks. When we're investment bankers, Jessica said, we won't ever take charity, and we'll give ten bucks to homeless men.

I would die, Jean said, if I were in my forties and a waitress. Did you see the huge veins on her legs?

It's worse if you carry trays, Jessica said. We don't carry trays. And we're just doing it for one summer. Next summer we'll have our internships.

Her veins are gross, Jean said.

I feel bad for her, I said. She has two kids.

She could have had two abortions, Jean said.

Jean! Jessica said. Don't say that!

Jean rolled her eyes. Kidding, she said.

When we got home, we drank tea and watched a few shows, as we did every night before bed. When we woke up in the morning, we drank juice-water—we consumed nothing but juice-water all morning, for our health—and then we rested for hours on the white beach by the house, splashing occasionally into the lake.

AT FIRST Dina earned the most money, but soon the twins were each earning double and triple what Dina or I did. Dina didn't seem to notice; however, she didn't seem to notice much. She was a better waitress than the twins, but the twins had a secret weapon—their sameness. Halfway through a meal, a man would reach out a fat arm, cup a shoulder in his moist hand, and say, Honey? Jean? And Jessica would say, I'm

Jessica. But I can get something for you. What do you need?

The man's eyelashes would flutter, his mouth corners twitch, his lips press together and make a raspberry sound. He'd say: Are you twins?

Jessica would nod.

He'd nudge the others in the party, mostly doctors, lawyers, and dentists who'd grown little beards and come up from Massachusetts on motorcycles for the weekend. Twins, he'd say. Our waitresses are twins!

I knew it, another man would say modestly. I've been watching them.

Jessica would wait, in these moments infinitely patient, balancing empty plates in one hand, holding an empty wineglass in the other. Then the first man, patting a tender, suncharred face, would say, Are you identical?

By the dessert course, half the table would be able to tell Jean and Jessica apart, because they would have been served by both, and they would have pulled the tale of the twins' aspirations from them. They would have handed the twins their phone numbers, shocked that the twins also liked golf, also liked boating, and also liked to water-ski, and made the twins promise to call them, so that they could do these things together, and those in the party who'd been able to distinguish—that one's bigger, that one's got slightly larger lips—would lord it over the others, saying, It's obvious, if you know where to look, and then they'd leave the twins an enormous tip.

The twins serviced all their tables together and pooled their tips—they called it their mutual funds, their honey pot, and the fruit of their sweat. At each night's end, when Dina was cleaning the kitchen, they'd count up loudly in the hall nearby.

It wasn't long before Dina pulled us aside. She said we needed to start getting to work on time. She'd been doing all the prep work. Also, were we stupid?

Because we'd been taking her parties' dinners and serving them to ours, whenever ours had ordered the same thing, and so her parties got their dinners late.

She's just jealous, Jessica said, in the car on the way home. Because she gets shitty tips.

I'd give her a shitty tip, too, Jean said. I'd tip her zero dollars.

I wouldn't, Jessica said. I'd never tip any waitress less than twenty percent. Because waitresses work hard.

All I know is this, Jean said: Dina has no right to yell at us.

She had a point though, I said, about us taking her dinners.

I'm sorry, Jessica said, but I don't think getting your dinner late is a big deal. Whenever I have to wait for my food, it tastes more delicious!

Dina was divorced and had two kids, a boy and a girl. The boy was sick. I didn't find out with what because I didn't ask. I just knew the boy was in the hospital, had been there a few months. One night when we were in the kitchen chopping vegetables, she dragged her wallet out. The kids were maybe eight and ten. The boy was chubby, had greasy brown hair, and was wearing a blue velour shirt. He was missing a tooth. The girl's hair was gray and her right eye was rolled toward her nose. I wanted to ask Dina why her daughter had gray hair. Instead I said they were cute. Dina got an olive glow on her face and said she thought so too. Then she put the wallet back. She might have liked them but she couldn't have hung out with them much, because some days she worked lunch then dinner and others she worked dinner and cocktailed after in the bar and lounge. When she cocktailed she wore a red bow in her hair. She'd take her last table in the dining room around eight. She'd do her side work, find the twins, and ask them if they needed anything else, and after she did the six things they wanted her to do, she'd put on lipstick, stick the red bow on, and go in the bar.

When I thought about Dina and her kids, I felt sad. But I thought about them only when I spoke to her and luckily we didn't talk much.

IN JUNE my tuition bill arrived and I put it in my tip box. I was worried about money, mostly because I was not a good waitress. I tried—I'd chant, Redhead wants prime rib with pilaf, blondie gets rib with potato, dickwad gets teriyaki with potato, nice guy veal with pilaf, but by the time I got to the kitchen, everything was jumbled in my head. As soon as I had six parties, I was swamped. A few times I asked the twins to help. They each said I should ask the other. The twins were never flustered, because they worked together and because they had a strategy: sacrifice. Whenever they had too many tables, they picked the party they thought would tip the least and ignored them until they'd taken care of everyone else. Later they'd explain to the sacrifice how busy they'd been, and the sacrifice would forgive them. I saw the strategy's merits but lacked the resolve to do it myself, and as a result I was flustered a lot.

By the end of June, Boris said things had to change. Did I know how many complaints he'd had about me? Did I want to guess?

I don't know, I said. Three?

Keep guessing, he said.

I don't want to, I said.

Then consider this your warning, he said.

ONE WEEKEND the twins' parents showed up at the house and held a barbecue for their friends. I met the twins' parents in the kitchen, where I'd come to get a snack. They hugged me, welcomed me, and told me to help myself to whatever was in the fridge. The door to the wide deck was open and I could see the friends outside, playing croquet on the lawn. I was about to thank the twins' parents, when Mrs. Serrano turned and said that while they were here, why didn't we settle up on the rent?

I must have looked confused, because Mr. and Mrs. Serrano said, more or less simultaneously: the summer's rent. Mr. Serrano named an amount. Then he put his hand on my shoulder. He seemed embarrassed for me. It's a modest rent, he said.

It wasn't. But I went up to my room, opened my tip box, and piled up my tips. When nothing was left, I brought the pile down. Mr. Serrano stared at the stack and said he'd been expecting a check. Then he said he'd make do. He took the pile and went back to the sunroom, where he'd been eating a peach cobbler, to count. I walked down to the beach. The twins were resting on it. Their long brown bodies were shimmering on one huge purple towel and the gold ends of their dark hair were flicking at their chins. I sat down and stuck my hands in the sand. I said I hadn't known I was paying rent.

You weren't, Jean said. I mean, we didn't want you to. But when we were presenting the idea to our parents, of you living with us, we threw it in, like, to sweeten the pot.

Jessica's eyes were wide. To make the pot a little sweeter! she said.

They must have seen a sour look on my face. Not only would I not make a killing, I realized, I might not break even. And then I realized something that shocked me: the twins would become investment bankers, after all.

Jean touched my shoulder. You would have paid rent anywhere else, she said.

So, Jean said. Do you want us to help you a little bit, with the rent?

We didn't know it would be a problem, Jessica said.

Jean poured some oil on her stomach and rubbed it in firmly. Maybe we can talk to our parents, she said. To get them to lower the rate a bit, for the second half. She looked at me. How about that? she said.

I STARTED WORKING lunch shifts in addition to dinner ones. This meant I spent my days with Dina. I didn't mind working lunch, because Dina refilled my customers' waters and bussed my tables. I told her not to, but she did it anyway. I'd realized she wore the same black shorts every day. They said "Tiger Wear" in a red triangular logo on the back, and had pleats in the front that accentuated her hips. When I asked how she kept them clean, she said she washed them at night in her bathroom sink. But I didn't feel bad for her, because she liked her job and was good at it. She had a lot of regulars, old people who tipped her ten percent. Her favorite was a Swedish couple. They must have been seventy-five, but they came in every day at noon, ordered six scotches and two prime ribs with pilaf, and ate the whole thing. Occasionally they ordered veal as a third dish, and offered Dina the chunk left, and Dina said she looked forward to eating it. They tipped her five dollars no matter what. I thought that was good, until I found out what their bill was. Then I thought it sucked.

Dina shrugged. They're old, she said.

But they drive a Mercedes, I said.

She stared at me. They're my customers, she said.

The next day Dina called in sick. I served all the regulars. They all seemed to know Dina well, and they all made me stand at their table while they talked about her: how she was so nice, how her son was ill, and how she had huge hospital bills because she didn't have health insurance. The Swedish couple gave me a lecture about America that ended with the conclusion that Sweden was superior because in Sweden the streets were sparkling clean and everyone had health insurance, and I nodded because I thought if I did they'd tip me well. They left me two dollars and fifty cents.

•   •   •

I WAS WORRIED about money, but my waitressing did not improve. No matter how fast I ran through the restaurant, I couldn't manage to get my parties what they needed when they needed it. One night Boris said he wanted to talk to me in the bar after work. In the bar he made me a drink. Then he said I was no good in the restaurant.

I told him I'd do better. I said I'd been memorizing the menu. But he shook his head. He said some people didn't have the brains to waitress. He said his restaurant was a dining establishment. He said he himself had seen me hold up a steak dinner and ask a table of twelve to hand it down the table to the person who'd ordered it.

Okay, I said. I'll stop doing that.

He shook his head again, and put his arm around my back. I like you, he said. He had a habit of smiling like he'd just heard a secret. He was doing it now, and his teeth were narrow and long. I think his gums had receded.

I like you too, I said.

The twins, he said—they're brats. Spoiled rotten. I don't even want them here next summer in fact.

I said I thought they had some internships lined up.

He didn't seem to hear what I'd said. He said the twins were vicious girls. Then he squeezed my shoulder hard and said that the twins had started life on third base and no one would ever look at me twice, the way people looked at them.

Maybe if there were two of me, I said. I was kidding, but I guess he didn't realize that, because he said, No, they still wouldn't. Then he said he needed a cocktail waitress. Dina had been doing it. Between me and him, she was better in the dining room. He finished his beer. God love her, he said, but she's too old to wear a bow in her hair.

I said I didn't want to take Dina's job. Boris stared. He said I wasn't taking her job, because he was giving it to me. He said I was lucky to have a job, the way I sucked in the dining room, and that Dina wasn't my concern, she was his.

Anyway, he added, she needs to spend time with her kids.

In the bar I did well. It was easy—all I had to do was write down the drink orders, carry the drinks over, collect the empties, and get my tips. The bar's triptych of glass walls faced the lake, its dark expanse and the pine-studded islands in its gray distance, and even though I often arrived before the sun had set, somehow the bar was always dim and I moved through it with the buoyancy and power of dreams. When I got home the first night, it was two a.m., and the twins were watching TV.

I wouldn't want to cocktail waitress, Jessica said.

No offense, Jean said.

He asked us if we'd work in the bar, you know, Jessica said. But it seems gross.

Anyway, Jean said, we knew *you* needed it.

The next night I saw Dina in the bathroom at the restaurant. It was nine o'clock, time for me to start work and for her to go home, but she wasn't dressed to go home. She was wearing a shiny purple shirt and a tight black skirt, and was leaning across the counter and putting on purple lipstick. I thought maybe no one had told her she'd been fired from the bar. I felt embarrassed. Before I could back out, she waved me in.

The purple lipstick was smeared above her lip, and her right hand was shaking a bit. She said she had a date—her first in eight years. She said the guy wore silver chains on his neck and worked at the dog track, but that other than that, he seemed nice. He'd told her she looked a bit like this Italian film star, one people used to tell her she looked like sometimes. She brushed a hand through her hair and repeated the star's name. I'd never heard it before. She added that the woman had been in a famous Western with Charles Bronson once, and I pretended to know who Charles Bronson was.

Good luck on the date, I said.

She thanked me. Then she shoved her stuff in her purse and asked me if I was working in the bar. I said I was. Whatever Boris had told me, she said, it wasn't true. I apologized, but before I could finish, she said to forget it. I was just a kid, she said, anyway. I didn't decide shit.

WITHOUT ANY SHIFTS in common, the twins and I barely talked. I wandered through their house during dinner hours, when the twins were at the restaurant, feeling like a thief or a guest. I looked through their closets, tried on their clothes, and ate tiny bites of their food. Then I smoked cigarettes and watched TV, until it was time for me to leave for the restaurant, and for them to come home and watch TV.

In mid-July the twins drove to the mall in the southern part of the state, near the college, and spent a few thousand dollars on clothes for the fall. When they got home, they brought the clothes to their room, laid them out on their beds, and told me to come see. I particularly admired one sweater, a gray cashmere one with a soft turtleneck, and I was rubbing the fabric between my fingers, pretending the sweater was about to go over my head, when I saw the price tag.

I said something stupid.

Jean looked annoyed. She explained that the clothes were an investment because they could wear them to work at their internships. She added that it was worth it to spend money on clothes you loved. If you wear a two-hundred-dollar sweater ten times, Jean said, that's twenty bucks a wear. But if you buy a crappy sweater for forty dollars and you only wear it once, that's forty bucks a wear. So expensive sweaters are cheaper than crappy ones.

I fingered the sweater. Its incredible loveliness reminded me I didn't have tuition money for the fall. I wasn't good at college—the social part, the academic part, any of it—but I wanted to go back.

Hey, I said. Did you ever ask your dad about reducing the rent?

The twins looked at each other.

Now is not a good time, Jean said.

Timing is everything, Jessica said.

We didn't want to tell you this, Jean said, but our dad's stocks are not doing well.

He got bum advice.

That's why he didn't stay up here this summer, because he really needs to concentrate on his stocks.

Nothing is certain, Jessica said.

We're not getting our new car this summer, Jean said. That's certain.

We've been cutting corners, Jessica said.

We're working hard, Jean said. We're really shopping for bargains.

Jessica took the sweater from me and held it against her breasts. Worrying about money is awful. I can't wait until we're bankers! We're going to help people invest!

Jean tapped my shoulder. There's no better way to help people, she said, than to help them invest.

I ASKED Boris to give me more shifts, and he said that as a favor, he'd let me work dinners again. One night dinner was slow, and the twins, Dina, and I spent most of the night on the back step smoking cigarettes. We worked up a good feeling talking about how hard the work at the restaurant was. When the good feeling wore out, the twins stared pensively into the dark. Eventually, Jessica touched Dina's hair.

I can't believe you've been waitressing fifteen years, she said.

Dina said it wasn't bad.

It's kind of bad, Jessica said. I mean, we only get two dollars and twenty-five cents an hour.

Plus tips, Dina said.

Yeah, Jean said. But we have to sing happy birthday to doofuses, and the benefits suck.

There are no benefits, Jessica said.

Dina shrugged. Once I got a Christmas bonus, she said.

How much? Jessica said.

Jean poked her.

Ow, Jessica said.

Dina's elbows were on her knees. It was generous, she said.

Later that night, when the twins and I were watching TV, I told the twins about Dina's kid being sick. I told them about her hospital bills and how she'd been angry when I'd taken her place in the bar.

I'm sorry, Jean said, but if someone wants health benefits, they should really work at Vollman's Mart, because Vollman's Mart gives health benefits.

I like Dina a lot, Jessica said, but no one's forcing her to be a waitress.

What do they get paid at Vollman's Mart? I said. Don't they get like five dollars an hour?

Jessica changed the channel to the late show.

Everyone has to start somewhere, Jean said.

I'D BEEN WORKING in the bar a few weeks when Boris said he wanted to talk to me after work. The carpet had needed vacuuming that night, and I wasn't done until two thirty. When I was done I was tired and hoped he'd forgotten about our talk, but he came in once I finished and stood at the bar.

I've been thinking, he said.

He sat down next to me. I felt nervous, though I didn't know why.

What I thought is this, he said. He put his hand on my leg. You could spend the night on my boat with me, he said, tomorrow night. He said, looking away from me, that it wouldn't have to be a big deal. It would be a relaxed time, and he'd bring champagne. He looked at me. His white curls were damp, and his face was hot pink.

I could use the company, he said. And I'd give you something for it. I know you could use extra cash.

I don't know, I said. What I meant was no. The glass in my hand felt slippery. I wanted extra cash. But I didn't think I could do it.

I'll pay you a thousand dollars, he said.

Oh, I said. The money was staggering. But there was no way I would do it.

All right, I said.

THE NEXT NIGHT at ten o'clock I was folding napkins in the waitress station when Boris came up behind me, pressed his stomach against my back, and wrapped his arms around my chest. It seemed unfair, as we weren't on the boat. The twins had left to go home—I'd told them I had a date with a guy I'd met, and they'd stared, and then shrugged, and left—but

Dina was still in the kitchen, cleaning the machines that the twins had supposedly cleaned. Boris whispered something about us both having a really good time. When he whispered, I turned around and saw the white hairs tufted on the pads of fat beneath his chin. He was smiling gently, his mouth half open. His breath smelled like peppermints and soured milk.

Excuse me, I said. I walked to the bathroom. I locked the door and sat on the toilet. On the toilet I tried to think about the thousand dollars. Thousand dollars, I thought, thousand dollars. But it didn't work. I didn't want to go on his boat. I knew I was behaving badly. I'd been taught not to back out of commitments. But I also wasn't sure why I'd said yes in the first place. It seemed stupid. If I didn't go back to school this fall, I could go back the next. I bit my nails. I recounted the tips I'd made at dinner. I counted three times. It wasn't much. But I felt sure I was getting better as a waitress. I put my tips in my apron and went out to the dining room. Boris was sitting at a table.

I said I didn't think I could make it.

He was angry. He stood up and yelled in the empty dining room that I'd wasted his night but that he wouldn't let me waste his night. Then he yelled some other things, about how he'd brought champagne from home and bought a new portable radio. Boris was swaying, and there was beer spilled on his shirt. I said I was sorry. He said he didn't care if I was sorry or not. I went back to the bathroom and stayed there awhile. I counted my tips a few more times. Then I went into the kitchen to ask Dina for a ride. It was late, and I'd thought perhaps she would have been gone, but she was there. She had her black coat on, and all her things in a bag. When I asked her for the ride, she stared. Her black hair was pulled back, her face looked gaunt, and she had the purple lipstick on. She didn't answer right away. When she did she just said, Call a cab.

THE NEXT MORNING when I came downstairs, Jean was eating a muffin at the kitchen table and Jessica was making tea. They said, in gentle voices, that they were glad I'd come home. Then they said that I should probably live somewhere else.

But the day was bright, and by our third hour on the beach together, they'd hugged me, forgiven me, and told me they didn't want me to leave.

We're not stupid, you know, Jessica said. Especially when it seems like someone gross asked you to do something gross, and it seems like you said yes, and then it seems like you changed your mind.

I knew you wouldn't do it, Jean said. I was just mad you considered it. And I wasn't mad, it was more I was concerned for your health.

Your mental health, Jessica said.

Not to mention your soul, Jean said.

Sometimes times are hard, Jessica said. But you still have to play the game right.

I nodded. Then I lay down on one of their towels, drank a bottle of their juice-water, and put some of their suntan lotion on.

At three o'clock, Jean went up to the house, and when she came back, she was yelling, Yahoo! Yahoo!

Jessica wriggled up onto her elbows and shaded her eyes. My sister's lost her mind, she said.

Jean yelled, Our dad's stocks are healthy again!

Yahoo! Jessica said.

Healthier than they've ever been!

Jessica turned to me. He was really worried, she said. He was so worried he could barely do number two.

And we're getting our car! Jean said.

Jessica's hands shot up. Yahoo! she yelled. Yahoo, Yahoo, Yahoo!

And, Jean said, I saved the best for last. She looked at me. Are you ready?

I nodded.

He reduced the second half of the summer's rent! He cut it right in half and then he cut it in half again!

That's terrific, I said.

Jean touched my arm. I told you not to worry, she said.

THAT NIGHT we arrived late to the restaurant. Dina was setting the tables for dinner, and her white shirt had the same patch of dried grenadine on the pocket that it had had on it the night before. She was walking funny, taking tiny steps around the room, walking without moving her hips. Also, it looked like someone had punched her in the mouth.

In the kitchen, Jessica's eyes went wide. Wow, she said.

Jean nodded. I don't feel bad for her, she whispered.

Jessica put a hand on Jean's.

That night Dina was slow serving customers and she got stiffed twice. Boris stayed in the kitchen, and didn't get drunk while he cooked or yell at us for not picking up our meals right away. He mostly stayed in the back, chopping things.

The next day I came down with the flu. I was sick for a week. When I recovered, the twins told me that during my absence, the Swedish couple had come in to eat lunch at the restaurant and Dina had told them to get out. According to the dishwasher, the Swedish couple had simply walked into the dining room, and Dina had told them to get out. She'd also said other things. Boris, who'd been listening from the kitchen, came in and made Dina take the rest of the day off. Then he served the Swedish couple their meals himself, and gave them their drinks for free. The dishwasher, who'd listened from the hall, said the Swedish couple hadn't been angry at Dina, and that they'd even argued on Dina's behalf—they'd said that a child's illness could make anyone crazy, and that they'd each gone crazy several times themselves for less compelling reasons, and that therefore Dina should be forgiven. Boris had told them not to think about it. She already was, he said.

Soon after Dina was let go from the restaurant, he took me aside. The twins had gone back to the college, I'd stayed on to finish the season's last few weeks, and the Christmas Inn seemed different without them—familial. Boris said a lot of things had happened that summer, and that he hoped he and I were okay. I nodded. He said Dina had wanted to leave the restaurant. I nodded again. He'd employed her four-teen years, he said. But sometimes people needed changes in scenery, and not all business relationships lasted forever. Plus, lately—his finger rose into the air and made a little circle near his head. I nodded. He thrust an envelope into my hand. The envelope had some paper in it, but I couldn't tell if it was money, or a long letter. Boris wished me well at college. His T-shirt had hardened crusty yellow armpits, and he looked tired. But he smiled. I hope you also know, he said, that whatever happens at school, you can always come back here. He put his arm around me and squeezed. He said, We'll make a place.

TO THE INTERSTATE

I COULDN'T BELIEVE we were getting away, my friend and I—sister, if you like. She was my sister. Somehow she'd gotten a car. It was one of those twenty-year-old Chevrolets or Lincoln Town Cars, it was like a boat, by which I mean I can see why people say those cars are like boats. The outside was cream with teak paneling, the seats were pale leather and somewhat cold even though the sun was shining, and the inside was big and tall enough to climb around in. I'd been on a boat once, and it had flown up and down the river beyond my control.

My sister picked me up on a street downtown, not a street near the home, so we were really getting away. For years I had written her letters, begging her to help me get out. I never doubted she would. We'd always helped each other no matter what. When she lived in the home, she argued with anyone who wanted to hit me and sometimes she combed my hair. And before we were in the home, when she shot the man, we said I did it. That was her idea, because I was younger. We both wanted him dead. And I probably would have done it myself, if I wasn't so scared of him and if I wasn't only six. I didn't mind, because for so long we were together in the home. Then she got out. She was gone. I waited as long as I could. Then I wrote letters. They weren't very good letters, but they expressed my desire that she help me get out of the home. When she didn't answer, I wrote more letters. Eventually she wrote, Don't contact me again. I wrote very small, short letters. She wrote, Don't write me again. Then I wrote that I would really rather die than stay in the home and she said that she would get me to the interstate. All we needed to do, she said, was get me to the interstate. I'd jumped from the roof, taken the dog path, and waited downtown near the gun store, where she'd told me to wait. Now I was sitting in the back. She was sitting in the front. I would have done anything for her. She was going fast. My idea was, we should go both far and fast, so we would really get away, but I noticed we were circling through the town. I didn't understand why.

I said, Do we need gas?

Yes, she said. We need gas.

I still hoped we might get out of town before we got the gas, but ahead was a red light, and that's when I saw the homeless men. There were two, by the light, and by the way they were standing I knew they'd try to get in the car. It's not that I hate homeless men and wish they were dead. It's more I know they hate me and wish I were dead.

Lock the door, I said. Then I pressed the lock myself. It was a long silver knob on the door. When I pushed it, it only went a little way down. My sister didn't say anything, but I felt safe because I thought the doors were locked. My sister had a determined look on her face. I thought she was determined we would get away. As soon as she stopped at the light, both homeless men walked toward the car. I felt scared, but I thought what would happen was that they'd try to open the door and be humiliated, because the doors would be locked. The door next to me opened. I wanted to close it but if I did it would shut on the man's groin and I knew that would make him mad. He got in the car. The other one got in the front.

These are the kind of locks where you have to push them down really far, my sister said, pushing one down really far to illustrate. We were still at the red light.

Thanks for not slamming the door on me, the homeless man next to me said. That would have hurt.

No problem, I said.

You know those handicapped buses? he said.

I nodded.

Well, he said, now they have doors that open up really suddenly, so all the handicapped people trying to get inside get knocked on their asses.

I nodded. He wasn't handicapped but I guessed he was probably friends with a lot of handicapped people, because he was homeless.

The light turned green and my sister took off. She was going really fast now, and finally we were beginning to drive through the town. We were flying along the dark two-lane road that passes the town hall, the old fire station, and the abandoned ski area, and the leaves of all the old trees were hanging above and blocking the sun overhead, a pale sun going down. The homeless man up front was having a conversation with my sister about something that had happened to him when he was homeless. The one who'd been next to me was moving around the car.

Look, I said to my sister, even though she was clearly having a conversation with someone else, we've got to get rid of them.

How? she said.

Both men looked at me. The tall one, who was telling my sister a story, had stiff red hair all around his face and a long wrinkled white nose. He was thin and wearing jeans and a red plaid shirt. The one who'd been next to me had a squat yellow face, yellow hair, and tiny lips the size of baby lips.

I crawled to the front of the car. Look, I said, to the one with the red hair, we have things to do.

We do? he said.

No, I said. My sister and I have things to do.

Oh, he said.

So we're dropping you off, I said.

Okay, he said. He rubbed his long white nose. Then he pulled his red beard.

My sister looked back at me. She said, Is it okay if we drop them off near the home?

No, I said. No way. We're not going near the home. We're dropping them off downtown.

So she turned around and drove back downtown, slowed by the village store, and pulled over in front of it. They got out. They didn't look at me. They just stood as if waiting, facing the road, with their hands in their pockets.

Drive, I said to my sister, and she drove. We're getting out, I said. We can't stop for any more lights.

All right, she said.

We need to go fast, I said.

All right, she said.

I was worried. Already time had passed, and at any minute I expected to see squad cars blocking the road and signs telling us to stop, or telling people to stop us; and it might have been, although I hoped it wasn't, already too late to get onto the interstate.

Don't worry, my sister said, and she began to drive fast and circle through the town.

I want to get out of town, I said.

All right, she said.

But up ahead was the light, the same one as before, and the homeless men were waiting by it.

Don't stop, I said.

All right, she said. But I do have to slow down.

I locked the door. The lock was the kind where you push one and they all go down, and this time I pushed the lock all the way down. But when the car slowed down at the light, just at the moment when I expected the homeless men to be humiliated, they opened the doors and got in.

The locks don't work, my sister said.

The tall one was next to her again, and the squat dumb-looking blond one with the tiny lips was next to me. I say dumb-looking, but he looked dumb in a sly way, as if he'd already pulled several over on me.

Thanks for letting me in, he said.

All right, I said.

I knew I couldn't say anything else because he was already in the car. I was angry at my sister for slowing down at the light, and for not being a good enough driver to get us away from the homeless men.

Can we at least get out of town? I said.

Sure, my sister said, we'll get out of town, but we need gas.

Oh, I said.

I didn't have any money. Also I didn't want to get gas, I wanted to get out of town; but I knew the car wouldn't work without gas, and already it was slowing down, like it needed gas.

I have a dollar, the tall redhead said, and he put his hand in his pocket and withdrew a dirty dollar from his jeans.

I have another dollar, the sly dumb-faced man said.

All tolled, the homeless men had three dollars and fifty cents. We used it to buy gas. I had a plan to get in the driver's seat at the gas station and take off with my sister before the homeless men got back in the car, but they were quick and got back in the car before I could do it. Also they were grinning at me as if they'd known what I'd been planning to do, and they probably did.

All I wanted to do was get on the interstate. But a lot of time had passed, and now, I knew, it might be too late.

Look, I said to the homeless men. You need to get out. You don't belong in the car.

The dumb, sly-faced one looked at me.

We don't? he said.

No, I said.

Okay, he said, we'll get out of the car.

My sister kept driving.

But we won't get out of the car, he said, because we're homeless.

I don't care, I said. You don't live here.

We don't live anywhere, he said.

Die then, I said. But not in this car.

We won't die, he said. We don't do that. We're homeless, but we're not dead.

We were driving along the same street as before, the one with the trees that hung over the road and blocked up the sun, and it wasn't a road that led to the interstate.

They paid for the gas, my sister said, and I saw that her hand was on the tall one's shoulder. Plus, she said, they're already in the car.

Well don't drive here, I said, because the sky was dark and the crows were hauling by overhead and the road we were on led to the top of the abandoned ski area. Drive somewhere where it's light, I said.

It's too late, my sister said again.

She was still in conversation with the taller, more handsome, redheaded homeless man about some event that happened to him years ago and I realized that while I had been busy trying to save us, I should have been trying to make friends. My sister is a wuss and will be nice to anyone who has a knife to her throat, whereas I am more honest and will tell the truth. I don't know why I do that; perhaps because of where I am from, which is the coldest part of New England. My sister is from there too, but since she left the home and lived somewhere else, she had escaped. I wanted to tell her what a liar she was, and how unfair it was that she was making me look like the only one who was afraid, but it was pointless to say that because the knife was already in the dumb-looking one's lap. It wasn't too big—it was only as long as the top half of his leg—but it was wide.

As soon as I noticed the knife, the tall redheaded man looked back and said, I think not all four of us can get onto the interstate.

The dumb-looking one looked at me. Sorry, he said.

My sister was still driving up the old wooded hill that led to the back of the abandoned ski area and she was looking forward without saying much, I think because she had known all along everything that was going to happen. Or maybe she'd wanted to save me, and thought it might not be too late. We had been sisters ever since we were born and it was in her nature to help out anyone she could, so that might have been the case. But now the tall redheaded homeless man had his hand on her arm and he was pointing toward a dirt road in the pines.

I like your sister, the sly, dumb-looking one said.

I nodded.

There really wasn't time, my sister said.

We could have driven faster, I said.

I drove pretty fast, she said.

In circles, I said.

At least she drove, the redheaded one said.

My sister kept driving. That's it then, I said, trying to be casually funny, I give up on the interstate. I was planning to jump out of the car. My sister pushed a button. The button was on the dash. After she pushed it, I tried to open my door.

Door doesn't work, my sister said.

It worked before, I said.

Temperamental, she said.

You pushed a button, I said.

She shrugged. She was very beautiful. She had long dark hair and was pale and thin. I'm only doing this, she said reasonably, because I want to live.

What?

She looked straight ahead.

They threatened you? I said. I meant them, the people in the house that she'd helped me escape.

Well no, she said. They didn't. But I just knew they'd be happy if I did it.

Oh, I said.

All those letters, she said. Wah wah wah. You should have shut up and waited it out.

I know, I said. All those years, I'd never realized how annoying my letters were. As I said, my sister had been in the house for a long time herself, but she'd waited it out and then scrambled around and led a miserable life, and now she had a pretty good position in the state, and I had thought she could help, even though by writing the letters I knew I was reminding anyone who happened to read the letters that once we lived together in the house.

Sorry about the letters, I said.

She looked out the window. She watched the firs fall past and the clustered black dots in the triangular valleys below. You always have a problem, she said. You need to buck up. I'm not even your sister.

You're not? I said.

No, she said.

We came to the top of the hill. The road was a dirt path. She parked next to a pine. I guessed no one had alerted the police after all, about our escape. My sister got out with the redhead and told the sly, dumb-looking one that they were going to find a spot.

He nodded.

Stay with her, my sister said. Then she walked with the redhead toward the woods.

The dumb-looking one slid closer. What are you thinking? he said.

I was thinking about my moves. I had three, but none of them was very good. Plus, the knife was on his lap. His blond hair was damp and his lips were pursed. He wasn't touching the knife but he was looking at me, and when he looked at me I knew that I was slow and he was fast. While I was thinking, I heard a shot in the woods. When I heard the shot I felt a gladness in my heart, because I don't like homeless men. Then I felt sad because I guessed he'd wanted to live. I realized my sister would kill us all because she wanted to live. I looked at the dumb one. He was studying me.

I love you, I said.

You do? he said.

Yes, I said. Very much.

You love me? he said.

From the moment I saw you, I said.

If I find out you're lying, he said, I'll kill you myself.

I'm not, I said. I convinced him to start the car. I pointed out that we'd both heard a shot. I said that it was time to leave. He started the car and backed it up.

Will you marry me? he said.

I saw my sister's shape in the dark, walking toward the car.

Yes, I said.

Have kids? he said.

Oh yes, I said.

My sister's shape was running toward the car.

Kiss my lips, he said, and let me put my tongue in your mouth?

Oh God, I said.

You don't love me, he said.

I do, I said. I just hate to kiss.

Oh, he said. Then he tore out of there fast and put his damp hand on mine and we headed toward the interstate.

THE ALPINE SLIDE

THE FIRST SUMMER I was old enough to work, Jacques Michaud opened the alpine slide. The slide was ten miles from the lake, in the mountains. Over the years, various businessmen had leased it for a summer or two and failed to make it a success. But Jacques Michaud was from Canada, and maybe he thought that made a difference. Or maybe he hadn't heard or believed the stories of previous failures, or maybe he thought the economy had changed. At least that was what he said when he hired us, and the economists were saying it, too.

Originally, the place had been a ski area. Thus the lodge, a low, flat, brown-shingled building, and the chairlift, a forty-year-old contraption with shiny red metal slats for seats. The lodge was in a grassy valley and the mountain was covered with pines. It was beautiful. But the peak wasn't the highest in the state, and the slopes weren't the steepest. Sometimes people came from Massachusetts to ski, but mostly they drove right past, headed farther north, to the White Mountains.

After the ski area went bankrupt, someone saw the abandoned lodge and lift and decided to lay down the alpine slide, two parallel cement tracks, each a mile long, that began near the top of the chairlift and wound their way down the mountain through the trees, twisting and dipping over spills of glacial rock until they shot out into the flat fields of the valley. The sleds were plastic and had two steel runners on the bottom. When the brakes were all the way off they could go thirty miles an hour, slipping up the high sides on the curves and lifting slightly from the track on the dips. The ride was two minutes long and you flew down the mountain as you flew in dreams, through seemingly solitary woods that leaned in of their own accord to block out the blue above. It was unforgettable, beyond your control, and you believed you were about to die.

People said the ride was wonderful, but they also forgot that it existed.

In the late seventies, a businessman made the place into a theme park by adding a waterslide. He put a cafeteria in the lodge, a snack shop by the lift, and constructed a craft village, a row of six chalet-style huts where local artisans sold landscape paintings, goddesses carved from driftwood, and candles shaped like frogs. When that park failed, another businessman made a better park by adding the Cannonball, a man-size tunnel you slid through until you were shot out into a pool. The fiberglass tube scratched your ass, and the water that sprinkled down from above made you feel as if you were drowning. The ride was seven seconds long, uncomfortable, and without danger or pleasure, but women's bikini tops sometimes popped off when they hit the pool and, for a while, the Cannonball worked. Then the water park at Bear Beach opened its own Cannonball, and the slide shut down for good.

We had looted it. By "we" I mean all the local teenagers, though my own participation was minor and of a different nature, since I lived nearby and considered it mine. Behind my house, there was an old carriage road that went halfway over the mountain, and when I was twelve and thirteen I'd follow it to its dead end, near the top of the lift, walk down the abandoned slide, and enter the lodge through a broken window. Inside, I took good looks at the cheap white dinnerware and ashtrays scattered around the nubbly blue carpet, tapped my fingers on the stacked-up plastic tables, and inhaled the stink of beer and mildew and the eggy scent of old sex. There were wooden slope signs—TRIGGER, SPLINTER, BONEBREAK, and GUNROCK—on the walls, and faded pink maps of the ski area, the mountains, the lake, and the state. But what I liked best was to lie back on the hot slide and stare at the sun. Older kids threw parties in the parking lot at night, made bonfires in the acres of dirt, and had sex in the manager's office amid the mouse turds and dust, but they were never subtle or quiet and soon after they got there the police would arrive and shoo them away.

Jacques Michaud was only renting the park, but he used his own money to replace the broken windows and repair the lift. He tore up the old nubbly blue carpet and put down a new nubbly blue carpet and restocked the cafeteria with frozen burgers and hot dogs, cases of soda, and industrial sheets of Jell-O and chocolate cake. He whitewashed the bathrooms and shower huts and planted cheap, hardy, orange brushlike flowers all around the park. Then he polished his car, a black 1956 Jaguar Mark VII sedan, and made stops at businesses all around the area, chatting up owners and dropping off batches of shiny purple brochures. Toward the end of this he drove to the Exxon station where my father worked as a mechanic and asked him if he had any kids, preferably daughters, who could work at the slide.

I was fifteen, and a daughter, and my world was circumscribed. I was expected to earn not less than an A- in school. I ate dinner with my family every night at six and was in bed by ten. I was not allowed to ride in cars with boys. My parents had other rules, all with the same purpose: I could not be alone with a boy. I'd never been kissed. I longed to be kissed. I spent a lot of time at home, in my room. I was also shy, and when I spoke, sarcasm came out of my mouth.

But I could work. My father believed in work, and he was intrigued by Jacques, enough to go on at length about the park's likely failure. Too far from the lake, the motels. No one wanted a dry slide in summer. "He says he's Canadian," my father said. "But he doesn't have an accent. To me, that means he's brilliant. He seems like a good guy. But I just don't think there's any way he'll make money from the park."

I RODE MY BIKE to the interview. Jacques Michaud's Jaguar was parked in the dirt lot outside the lodge. My father had said it resembled a Rolls-Royce, but it looked like a hearse.

On the slope beyond the lot, gold grasses waved and the metal towers of the lift glinted white. The wires holding the chairs shimmered like mirages in the heat. A hawk floated in the sky like an ash.

The lodge was so dark that I couldn't see. But I smelled a cigar. Someone—Jacques Michaud, I guessed—said something from the corner. His voice was low but casual, as if he were utterly relaxed. He was sitting at a lunch table. He got up and pulled out a cafeteria chair and told me to have a seat. Then he sat back down. He had a dinner plate in front of him, with the remains of a ham sandwich on it, which he was using as an ashtray.

His skin was dark and his hair was white. Pure white. But he wasn't old—or he was, to me, but not enough to have white hair. He was forty, maybe fifty. It was hard to tell. His body was muscular—he was wearing shorts and a T-shirt, and his legs were brown, almost hairless, and thick.

I was shocked that he wasn't wearing a suit. I'd worn black polyester pants and a stiff white shirt, which was now wet from sweat, and I had had a lot of trouble pedaling my bike along the highway in my dress shoes.

"Would you like a cigar?" he asked. He waved toward the kitchen. "I have more in back." He took a puff, held it up, and read the tiny silver letters on the dark-red band. He squinted. "They're not illegal," he said. "But they're pretty good anyway."

I considered cigar smoking disgusting and lethal. But I was looking at him and considering having one when he said, "I was kidding."

I nodded stupidly.

He glanced at his watch. He hadn't seemed to look at me at all. "You're too young," he said. "But I'll hire you."

"You haven't even interviewed me," I said.

"Well," he said. He put the cigar on the plate. "You seem like an honest person to me. You look honest. And I met your father. He's a good man."

"He's good at fixing cars," I said.

He leaned forward. "That's important. It's important to fix cars."

I wasn't sure what to do with this. I felt as if he were saying something intimate. But he was talking about cars. My father was a shame between us, acknowledged and then forgotten.

What I understood then was that the world was contriving in secret, with swiftness and accuracy, to keep Jacques Michaud from making the park a success. But, Herculean, he was lifting it onto his shoulders. I was invited to be with him while he lifted it. Perhaps I could help.

I liked how he looked. His white hair curled over his broad forehead a bit, which made him seem oddly boyish. He had a wide, hawklike nose, a strong chin, and full pink lips.

"Let's say I interview you," he said. "I've hired everyone I need. The law says you're too young to work moving machinery. That means you can't load sleds on the lift, top or bottom. So why should I hire you—what can you do?"

My spine straightened. "Well," I said. "I can stand at the bottom of the slide. I can also sit at the top of the slide and show people how to use their sleds. I know CPR. I could work at the waterslide." I listed other things. He listened without expression. "I suppose I could work in the cafeteria," I said. "Though I'd really rather work at the slide—"

"Stop," he said. "You're hired."

"Thank you so much," I said.

He put his cigar on the plate and came around to my side of the table. I stood up. I assumed the interview was over. His hand came out and I stared at it. "Shake hands," he said.

I did. His hand was large and warm.

"Now we're partners," he said. Then he gave me some forms to fill out and disappeared into the basement.

I was about to leave when he appeared at the top of the basement stairs. "Hey, Bowman," he said. "Do you know what I'm counting on to make the park a success?"

I shook my head.

"I'm counting on you," he said. "You are excellent. I've hired an excellent staff. And you will be excellent, too. I can tell."

NO ONE HE'D HIRED was over twenty-three, and most were eighteen. The other employees were the most popular people in my school, but because I was the youngest by far they accepted me as a kind of younger retarded sister. We were bonded by the fact that we all loved Jacques. He was the kind of man who was willing to make a group of kids his friends. This didn't mean that we weren't aware of an aura of failure about him, that we didn't sense that he was lonely and sad or feel glad that we weren't him. But he had given us jobs. He paid us more than minimum wage. And he did not require us to wear uniforms. The boys wore dark swim trunks of their choosing and the girls could wear whatever. Most wore bikinis. We were given fifteen-minute breaks every three hours, and during them we were free to ride the waterslide to cool off. The lodge had a bar in the basement that had originally been for skiers, which Jacques didn't open to the public. But sometimes at the end of the day, when the pink sun was lighting just the tips of the wheat around the parking lot and all the customers had left and we'd finished putting the sleds away and hosing the platforms down, he opened it for us.

I went once. The carpet was the same nubbly blue as the cafeteria's—only it hadn't been replaced—and the room had a long black bar, a bunch of barstools, and some wooden tables and chairs. I sat at a table with some other workers and listened to what they said. I was perfectly happy. The bar smelled like incense, grease, and nutmeg. The sun was coming in through the basement window and illuminating the glasses on the tables and the grains in the wood. I could see Jacques at another table. Every few minutes he'd say something, then he'd sit back and his hands would spread in the air. He was talking to Amy Goldman, who'd be a senior in the fall but was already eighteen because a virus had kept her out of school for a year. He was teaching her how to bartend. "At your natural speed," he said. "Don't rush."

She said, "One, two, three, four."

"Good," he said. "You're a slow counter. That means you count to three and a half. Then stop." She nodded.

"That's it," he said. "You never need to measure. You just count." He said something else I couldn't hear, and she laughed. Sometime later, I heard Jacques telling a story. I'd missed the first half. In the second half, a young airline pilot was excited about his new fiancée, who was riding in coach. Once the plane hit cruising altitude, he met up with her in the lavatory. Jacques paused. "And when the stewardess went into the cockpit to ask the pilots how they wanted their coffee," he said, "the old guy was asleep by himself."

"No one was flying the plane?" Amy Goldman asked.

Jacques smiled. "No one was flying the plane." Then he shrugged. "Autopilot usually does fine. In those days, all the airlines had a pretty late retirement age, and the old guy fell asleep a lot."

"So what happened?"

"They got fired," he said.

Someone asked him if he'd been the younger pilot.

"No," he said. He picked up his glass and drank. "The story just went around."

He went upstairs to use the bathroom then, and when he came back down he sat next to me. "Bowman," he said. He asked me how I was, and how I liked working at the slide. I said I was good, and that I liked my job. Then he put his hand on my shoulder and said that I'd better go home.

When I got home, I was grounded. From now on, my parents said, I would come home right after work. There was no reason to stay. I told them I'd just wanted to talk. "Talk at work," they said. "You can talk to those people all day."

So each night I pedaled home along the highway, almost swerving into the ditch every time a car came, and imagined I was back in the lodge telling stories, even though in real life I almost never talked.

I read books. My favorites were the ones in which young Victorian women were forced by adverse circumstance to have sex with swarthy highway robbers who were twice their age and had impeccable manners and great taste in jewels. On the front of these books, the women's shining satin bodices were being ripped apart not by the big-muscled highway robbers themselves, but by sheer spontaneous combustion, helped along by the women's rapid breathing patterns. The books were all the same. Once the robber gets the woman alone in his ramshackle but comfortable hideaway, which includes a big satin-pillow-filled bed, he looks around, notes the absence of the second bed, and says that if he were a gentleman, he would sleep on the floor. But he is not a gentleman.

She tells him he is disgusting, a villain, a scoundrel, that her father will discover the abduction and will take revenge, likely with dogs.

The robber finds this laughable.

"It is not in my nature to force you, Carlotta," he tells the woman once they are in the bed. "But I will have to kiss you, you know. . . ."

With one thick finger he compels her to look into his face. His black eyes are smoldering like burning bread. His lips are so rough they are cracked into segments.

"After all," he says, "I went to such trouble to abduct you."

"No," Carlotta whispers. "I loathe you . . . loathe you . . ."

Two brief pages later, she's pregnant and locked in a tower.

I prayed that something similar would happen to me.

JACQUES LIVED in an empty room in the lodge's basement, behind the manager's office. It had one small window at ground level, which he sometimes threw a blanket over. On the floor was a clock radio and a queen-size mattress. The only other furniture was a dresser full of T-shirts and shorts. On the dresser was a picture of a babe. An older babe, but a babe—a redhead with an angry look on her face. The woman was Jacques's dead wife. Or that was what we'd heard. Her death had left Jacques alone in the world. He missed her every day. He'd traveled all around the globe. Now he thought he'd settle down. He'd picked New Hampshire because he'd heard it was beautiful. Second only to Canada. He'd seen the park, and it had seemed like a great opportunity. A beautiful niche in the mountains. Cheap rent. He contacted the owners, and had them lend him the keys. He'd carried a sled up the mountain and ridden it down. He'd made up his mind right then. He didn't see how such an incredible feeling couldn't be a success.

We were not excellent workers, mostly because we were stunned by the pleasure of one another's company. Soon our legs became scraped from lifting sleds, and our arms grew sore and then muscular. Our skin turned gold. Our fifteen-minute breaks stretched to thirty. Instead of half price, our

snacks were free, because the snack-stand crew, a lower ech-
elon of workers who were trapped in grease and darkness,
offered them to us that way.

The waterslide had an office, a white cement room that
looked out onto the pool through a window, and in it was
a black vinyl chair that rolled on three silver wheels, the
fourth having been lost, some water-stained pamphlets on
how to perform CPR, and an enormous black stereo with
two cassette decks that played a joyous cacophony of Mega-
deth and the Beastie Boys. This office became the site of
passionate and private discussions, during which the partici-
pants leaned a chair against the door and propped a mat over
the window.

On the platform at the top of the lift, teenagers stretched
into strange nature-worshipping poses and smoked cigarettes. Their job was to tell customers to raise the safety bar,
to help them off the chairs, and to hoist the sleds from the
chair backs, but when no customers were visible they sat in a
circle on the platform and told dirty jokes and played cards.

The mountain crew was always thirsty and sending
someone down the hill for drinks. The waterslide crew was
thirsty and hungry, too. As the youngest, I was chosen, no
matter where I was stationed, to make the food run. Under
the yellow awning of the snack stand, I'd order three large
nachos with extra cheese, six raspberry slushies, three
cheeseburgers, and five chili dogs. The server would pack
everything into a shallow cardboard box, and I'd give him
the soft, ripped bills I'd collected. He'd push them back. On
my return along the sandy path to the slide, Jacques some-

times passed by, walking slowly, wearing shorts and an old polo shirt, tight under the arms. He'd look up and nod, appearing to see only me, not the box.

I wondered how he could notice so little. I guessed he was preoccupied. He'd hoped we'd have six hundred people a day, and we hadn't yet. He was always chatting up the customers and making lists of needed supplies, and every day at noon he drove to a different neighboring town to distribute brochures. He kept a few in the pockets of his shorts, and sometimes he'd absentmindedly shove them farther in, because the tips stuck out. He'd had them printed himself, and on the front was a picture of Amy Goldman. I could understand why. She was the most glamorous, if not the most beautiful, girl in school. Within a week of the park's opening, she was dating Dave Z., the assistant manager and second-oldest employee of the park. He was going back to college in the fall, and she had another year of high school, so by necessity it was a turbulent and passionate affair, one that touched us all. Dave Z. had blond hair and a deadly smile full of teeth. He never spoke to us except to tell us to do something, and then he called us kids. It seemed fitting and tragic that Amy Goldman should be his. She was a blond goddess—five foot eight with strong legs, a waist like a man's neck, and the largest breasts it was possible to have without their being too big. Her posture was as straight as if she were walking at sea. Her skin was bruised apricot, her nose hooked, and her eyes green. Her smile could make any of us agree to perform the dingiest tasks—spraying down the concrete floors of the bathrooms, for example, or cleaning up a shit someone had taken on the men's-room floor. At the waterslide, she always wore a red bikini, and when she leaned forward to blow her whistle or tell a child to move away from the bottom of the slide there was an ever so slight bulge of flesh beneath her breasts.

She and Dave Z. did it in the waterslide office on the black vinyl chair. They did it in the showers on a cloudy afternoon. They did it in Jacques Michaud's office, on his desk, when Jacques Michaud wasn't there.

Jacques Michaud was oblivious. He walked around the sandy paths of the park with his head down, looking for pieces of glass. When he looked up, he seemed to be staring at a lone house—the local millionaire's—on the pine-covered mountain opposite.

OCCASIONALLY, Amy and I worked together at the top of the slide. Where, because I couldn't work the lift, I spent a lot of time—in a high, sunny, sandy clearing, surrounded by white pines and hemlocks and scraggly junipers—showing the people who emerged from the path in the woods how to use their sleds. One afternoon, it was slow, and Amy and I were left sitting in the sun by ourselves. She was wearing her bathing suit to tan.

I asked her what the virus was that had kept her out of school for a year. She said the doctors had had about five different explanations and that none of them had made sense, that they'd tested her for everything, even syphilis. Sometimes her arm had been numb, or her leg, off and on, for a night or a day; and she'd felt tired. One doctor had told her that it was growing pains. Another had said that she was depressed. She laughed and said that it didn't matter now, because she was fine.

She took a carrot stick out of a Baggie and offered me one.

"It made me realize that I should study more," she said. "Once I get to college, I'm going to study all the time."

She tucked her hair behind her ears and smiled. Her cheeks were round when she smiled, and she suddenly seemed very young. I smiled, too, for no reason, and a bunch of kids came out of the woods with their sleds, laughing and shouting, then stood by the slide for five minutes arguing over who was faster. They made us count down for them so that they could race, in sets of two. After they left, it was quiet. Two dark-blue dragonflies sloped through the clearing. I stared at the red berries on the junipers, the shiny green leaves of the checkerberries below—and then I asked her when Jacques had taken the picture for the brochure. She said a few days before the park opened. I asked her if he'd paid her to do it. She shrugged and said that he'd offered, but she'd said no. She didn't see why he should. "It wasn't a big thing," she said.

"Did he take it himself?" I asked.

She stared at me. "Of course he took it himself. He's not a millionaire." She frowned a bit. "He was very sweet," she said. "It wasn't weird."

I nodded. Then she asked me if I had a boyfriend. I shook my head.

"Well, you're not missing anything," she said. "It's a pain in the ass."

I nodded.

She leaned back, and closed her eyes.

BY LATE JUNE, we didn't have six hundred people a day. We didn't have five hundred. For three days it rained, and when the sun came back the chairlift malfunctioned and for two days Jacques sold half-price tickets.

My father tallied the gross income from three hundred customers a day on the back of our electric bill, subtracting estimated employee incomes and making various other columns under an all-caps heading, "OVERHEAD," and concluded that Jacques couldn't be making a profit.

But I thought he was. He had an air of contentment. He spent every morning checking the mechanics of the slide, and he was especially careful about the sleds. He made the maintenance guys check every sled every day—Were the runners straight? Did the brakes work?—which seemed excessive, since each rider had to check the brakes before heading down, and you didn't need a brake. A ride without brakes was a wild ride. We'd all done it, and we all had slide burn as a result. It was a strange wound. Only the first few layers of skin, whatever portion had skimmed the slide—usually the knees, or the backs of the arms, or thighs—and the burns didn't bleed; they oozed pink fluid. They could be as large as a hand or as small as a dime, and they hurt, but only until the EMT in the emergency shack put the iodine on. Then they stung for an instant and pulsed for a few days. They faded to a slippery shine, a pale shade of lilac, and seemed to travel, so that months later you'd be looking for one, to show someone, and it would be somewhere else on your arm, somewhere different from where it had been. Or maybe you'd just remembered it wrong.

Jacques caught me pushing one of mine with a thumb one day when I was working at the bottom of the slide. The day was slow, and everything smelled like heat: the slide, my skin, the dirt that slid along the ground in the breeze. Jacques grabbed my arm, glanced at the burn, and said that it was pretty good. Then he stood next to me and looked around the park. A group of maintenance guys were shuffling by on their way to the sled-repair shack, where they got high between jobs. Jacques watched them go. His feet were spread wide in the dirt and he crossed his arms over his damp shirt. Then he asked me which one of them I had a crush on.

I looked at them. They were all gaunt, except for one, who had dark hair, a paunch, and a soft, dopey look. I shrugged.

"I know," he said. "I know."

I watched him walk off toward the waterslide. When he got there, he waved to the people by the pool, of which there were only two, because Amy Goldman and Dave Z. weren't present. Jacques stopped in front of the closed office door. The mat was over the window. He stood there, looking at the mat, for about ten seconds. Then he turned around. He glanced at the chubby, sunburned lifeguard who'd stood up from his stool out of nervousness. "Wrong office," he said.

He turned when he was halfway down the ramp. "If you see Dave Z.," he said, "tell him to stop by and see me."

Dave Z. wouldn't tell anyone what Jacques said that day. But after that he made small talk with the customers, cleaned his nails when he thought no one was looking, and said "Please" and "Thank you" when he told us to do something.

ON THE LAST DAY of June we had a hundred and thirty-two guests. Jacques stopped me as I was delivering a box of cheeseburgers to the waterslide. His face was red from heat, and the fabric under his arms was yellow. He gestured to the people waiting to ride the lift. "You see this?"

I nodded.

His hand dismissed the line. "You'll wish for this in July," he said. Then he tugged his baseball cap down, put his hands in his pockets, and trudged toward the lodge.

But when the Fourth came it was so humid that the air seemed tinged by the colors of people's clothes. Dewdrops formed on the slide, and every half hour two of us had to ride down pushing towels in front of our sleds with our feet to dry it off. We never closed unless we felt drops or saw lightning—so we were open, but no one came. That night the fireworks above the lake were blurry, and mosquitoes made a faint sound like the echo of a tuning fork.

It wasn't just us. The economy was strong, but our town was dead. The swarm of tourists that had arrived in past years hadn't materialized. The boardwalk at Bear Beach was quiet, the lake a vast blue. Lone motorboats buzzed by empty beaches. Our local news reported that the people who'd come to our town in the past, mostly from Massachusetts, weren't coming now because they had more money now and could go to Europe.

"I could have told him," my father said. "The alpine slide is just not a great idea. I'm not sure why he thought he could do what no one else could."

Jacques announced a tightening of the belt. He spoke about the difference between the behavior he'd seen and the behavior he wanted to see. He said that he thought we could work a little harder. He said it with perfect equanimity, and soon afterward Amy Goldman and Dave Z. quarreled. He was going back to college in a month. He was thinking about the future. He wanted to date other people. She gave him an ultimatum. Out of all or nothing, he chose nothing. Now when he spoke to her it was the same way he spoke to everyone else, to tell her to hose out the rest rooms. Their awkwardness would have affected us, but we were busy working hard, which was difficult, since it was quiet and there was little to do.

In mid-July, we each met with Jacques Michaud in his office to see if we'd get a raise. When I went in he was sitting behind his desk, a dinged-up metal one that had been in the basement office for at least ten years. He was smoking a cigar.

"I don't need a raise," I said. I told him I was worried about the park. I explained it stupidly, in detail. I was so nervous I was stuttering. He grinned.

"We're doing okay," he said. "We're doing all right. Don't worry about the park." Then he said something strange. He said I was the best worker he had. He said that I had the nicest smile. He said that I made customers feel happy they'd come. "Everyone should treat customers like you treat them," he said. "You think I haven't seen you, but I have. You work hard."

On my way out, he stopped me. "Come by after work and have a drink with us sometime," he said. "Stay and talk."

I wanted to. But from then on the gatherings were canceled, because the next day, a day when we were actually busy, a woman came down the slide with her face burned off. It was a beautiful morning, and an alabaster light had clapped down over the entire park. Mica gleamed on the sandy paths, and the upturned orange flowers were white at their tips. I was stationed at the bottom of the slide. I'd been telling people to hurry up and get off so that the people behind them could come down. The woman's sled was moving slowly. She was leaning forward, but she had no momentum and the sled just stopped fifty feet up the hill. I yelled at her to keep going, and then two sleds came down fast behind her and bumped her rear and her sled inched forward a bit. She looked up. Her cheeks, nose, and forehead were the red of semiprecious gems. She didn't move—she sat in her sled and stared ahead. A line of kids waited morosely behind her while I climbed up the hill. I helped her up and pulled her sled off the track. The woman walked with me quietly. She had short curly brown hair, thinning at the crown, and was stout. She was maybe thirty-five or forty. I asked her what had happened, and she said that halfway down the mountain she'd been thrown from her sled. She thought she'd hit something. I nodded, though I couldn't think what she might have hit. Her face was oozing the tiniest pricks of blood, as if from a cheese grater, and it made me nervous so I took her hand. "Don't worry," I said. "It usually disappears." But when we reached the EMT shack the EMT took one look and called an ambulance.

Jacques held a meeting. Most likely, he said, the accident had been caused by a rock in the track. This was an unforeseeable and bizarre circumstance. He was doing everything in his power to help the woman, he said. She was in the best hospital. She was comfortable. In a day she'd be able to go back to her job. There was no problem. However, to prevent future bizarre events, we would now wipe the track down twice in the morning, instead of once, and twice again in the afternoon.

Jacques said all this, but he didn't sound sure of it. He looked as though he hadn't slept.

He cleared his throat. The potential complication, he said, was a lawsuit. But he had visited the woman in the hospital, he had promised to pay for the surgery she'd need once her face healed, and she had said that she wouldn't sue. And he believed her. Did we know why?

Someone suggested that it was his charm.

"Come on," Jacques said. "I'm not that charming. Look at my face. See this face?" He gestured. His face was sweaty and red. "It's an ugly face," he said.

Someone said, "It's not like she was a movie star."

The guy who'd said it was a tall, sarcastic redhead who'd once, as a joke, asked me when I was going to go out with him. I'd treasured the question even though he'd walked off before I could answer. Now Jacques stared at him. The guy stared back. "I don't care," Jacques said. "And I don't want to hear anyone say that again."

"It's no one's fault," someone said. "It was an act of God."

Jacques spat on the floor. "It wasn't an act of God."

"Why not?"

He stared at us incredulously. "Because it was a rock. In the track."

No one said anything else.

He sighed. Then he put on his baseball cap. "This woman works at the Kmart," he said. "She lives in a trailer, she doesn't have a washer and dryer, and she's not going to sue because she's from New Hampshire. She's a local." He wiped his forehead. "Locals don't sue," he said. "It's those bastards from Massachusetts that sue."

TWO NIGHTS LATER, the woman was on TV. Except for holes for her eyes and mouth, her face was a swath of white cloth. She was sitting on a brown couch with her hands in her lap. The deflated folds of her stomach slumped over her jeans. She told the interviewer that her life would never be the same. The interviewer asked her if she was planning to sue. At first, she didn't answer. She just sniffed a lot. Then she said, "What do you think?" Then she said some things about how her children would look at her, then she started bawling and they cut the tape.

My father shook his head. He said that it was a shame. He said that he'd always been impressed with Jacques's initiative, he'd always liked the park, and it was a shame that a woman would destroy a good business with a lawsuit.

As soon as my parents were asleep that night, I climbed out my window. I wanted to warn Jacques Michaud. The woman was suing, and I thought if he knew he could do something, like pay her off. I felt sure that he'd want to do that. I put on sneakers, a turquoise-blue tank top that I thought I looked pretty in, and shorts for maneuverability. I swung from my window onto the sunroof, crawled down its steep shingles, and dropped ten feet onto the grass. Then I walked in the heavy dark over the pass. There were a few houses along the way, the houses of old people, but their lights had long since gone off. The moon was nearly full and the tops of the trees swayed blackly in the tar-blue sky. First warped pavement, then oiled dirt rose up under my feet. I stumbled every few minutes. As the road narrowed and became a path, mosquitoes whined by my ear and pines left pitch on my arms. My heart was beating fast. In my head I was already there. The whole basement was lit. Music was playing and people were laughing and drinking, looking lovely, all while forming a plan to save the park. When I arrived, they would welcome me and I'd come up with the solution, and while they would have been attracted to me before, now they would love me. By the time I started down the hill, tripping down the ghostly white slide, I had forgotten that I had no solution. Below, in the clearing, the lodge looked dark. There were only two cars in the lot. Little black things were swooping through the inky sky above the chalets.

When I tried the door, it was locked. I knocked. I could see a faint light through the keyhole. I knocked again. I called Jacques's name. The black bushes swayed by the basement windows. I walked along the perimeter until I reached the one with the light. I squatted down to peer through. In the room, Jacques's room, were two people on a mattress. They were wrapped around each other in a million ways. The man's hair was white, his body dark and thick. The woman's mouth opened in an expression of sorrow, her eyes narrowed, her hands grasped his hair, and she kissed him. It was Amy Goldman. Her blond hair was a gold light that filled the foot of space between her head and the pillow. I felt as if an army were marching through my heart, singing a terrible and joyous song. Jacques placed his hand behind her head and whispered something into her ear. I walked home.

WHEN I REPORTED to work the next morning, no one was there.

My parents made gestures at pity, and my older sister offered to get me a job at the motel where she worked as a chambermaid.

The next day, Jacques was on the front page of the local paper. Jacques Michaud, park operator, had skipped town, the article said, owing thousands in electric bills and evading the pending lawsuit of one Charlotte Blanc. In fact, he was not Jacques Michaud. He was Mike Vost, from Chicago, where he was wanted for tax fraud and for operating a bar without a license. As a side note, he had been running the park without insurance. The last person to have seen him was Harry, who owned Harry's Garage in town, and who'd bought his Mark VII Jaguar for four thousand dollars, at two thousand under book. The park was closed until further notice.

For two days I moped around the house. I refused to take the motel job. On the third day, my mother said she wanted me outside, so I put on sneakers and walked over the pass. I walked down the slide. I could see the black figure eights from when they'd greased it last. The Cannonball was dry, the huts of the craft village closed, and the lot, when I reached it, was empty. I tried the door of the lodge. It was open. Inside, nothing had changed. The slope signs were still on the walls. The kitchen hummed. In the freezer rows of beef patties were crusted with ice. In the fridge, the vats of Jell-O were growing hard. I walked out and around the back. A car was parked there with its trunk open. I was peering into the trunk when Jacques came out of the lodge. He was grinning. In the trunk, I could see a suitcase and a lot of loose, junky-looking clothes. He hugged me. He squeezed me tight. I didn't want him to let go. He let go. He pushed me away and crossed his arms over his chest.

"I'm not really here," he said.

I nodded.

"I had a few things to pick up."

I nodded.

He cleared his throat. "Look," he said. He stared at me. "I offered that woman five thousand dollars. It would have paid for her operation. I offered."

I evaluated this. I said, "Are you in love with Amy Goldman?"

He gestured to the car. "This is my new car," he said. "Like it?" It was tiny, a red hatchback, rusted all over. "It's kind of small," he said, "but I fit in it."

"It's all right," I said.

"Come here," he said. I stayed where I was. "The whole world is in love with Amy Goldman," he said. Then he said that he wasn't in love with her, but that he liked her a lot and was sure she'd do well in college. I asked him how his wife had died. I felt suddenly very bold and skilled at conversation, so I asked. He looked surprised, then sad. I thought he was going to tell me to fuck off. Instead, he slumped. After a minute, he said he'd screwed up the marriage and that she lived in Jacksonville, Florida, and was married to a tax attorney. Then he shrugged. "Come here," he said. "Give me another hug."

I did. I thought he might take me with him. I was ready to get into the car.

But he held me at arm's length.

"You're too quiet," he said. "The world won't come to you. You can wait as long as you want. It won't come to you. You can wait as long as you want. And then it will be gone."

THE NEAR-SON

I KILLED A NEAR-SON today. Naturally I did not tell my lover about it. But when I was at the clinic his ex-girlfriend was there and she recognized me, and when that snitch got home she called my lover on the phone and told him what I'd done. She probably snuck it in as if she didn't mean to let it slip. "Oh I saw Mona today at the clinic," she would have said. "You knew she was there, right? We chatted a bit—" and so forth. We hadn't even chatted a bit.

She walked out of the clinic as I walked in. She had on a silver sheaf and looked glamorous. In the exit she paused and I did too because she'd blocked my way. She took her sunglasses off and bobbed her chin at me. I guessed she had an idea who I was but that she wasn't sure, and I knew I should not bob back. But part of me thought: Maybe it means We're friends. I bobbed back. Her lip curled. She stepped aside and I said, Thanks! and went in and got it done.

When I got home I was thinking, Scot-free, scot-free! My lover was lying down on the couch with a compress on his head. The TV was on the sports channel, but he wasn't watching TV.

How was the mall? he said. But he said it in a dull, sarcastic voice, like he was dead.

I should have known then, but I didn't.

The mall was great! I said. I held up some pretend shopping bags, as if I'd almost bought a million things. Pretty expensive though, I said.

My lover looked at me with his narrow blue eyes, the ones that first convinced me we should really have sex.

My near-son died today, he said. I felt a tingle when you did it.

I knew I was in trouble then. So I hung my head to show I wanted to be forgiven. Even though he was making the tingle up. He got the tingle from his friends, because they all had stories about the tingles they'd felt when their near-sons were dead. Also, ever since his friends had found out they had even one near-son, they'd decided they each had a few dozen. To find out their real number, they multiplied each girlfriend they'd had by four, five, or six. The number came from a formula that involved a woman's height-to-weight ratio, how much money her parents made, and the width of her hips. My lover's friends liked to get together and drink French-roast and reminisce, as in, "I almost met my near-son today." They were all great friends. According to them, the way you met your near-son was, you felt the tingle and knew his spirit was close. Or if you were sensitive, you might see him full-blown, about seventeen or eighteen and about to wave before he vaporized—the only way to know it was him, besides being sensitive, was that he looked like you knew he would, which was a lot like yourself in your prime. The other way to see him was to see a real guy who resembled him, in which case you might confuse the guy for a spirit and say, "Hey near-son, wanna toss a few back?" and the guy would say, "Go screw."

I don't know why you did it, my lover said, or how you could. He adjusted the compress on his head.

I don't know either, I said.

But I had reasons. For one thing, I knew a son would cry all day. For another, I was low on cash. I worked hard as a waitress to support my lover and myself. My lover was an out-of-work fiscal analyst. But what he wanted to analyze, I wasn't sure, and neither was he. The economy was pretty bad. Sometimes my lover spent whole days sitting with his friends, also out-of-work analysts, eating potato chips and drinking beer and discussing how in these dark times, no one appreciated analysts. Mostly I didn't care though because his eyes were so blue and he made me forget myself in bed. I forgot myself a lot. But I made enough money to pay the taxes and buy us a lot of ham and bread. I think we both felt if we waited long enough, things would turn good. Everyone we knew felt that way. As in former times, people were waiting for a king to be born. It was said he would be a near-son who'd slip past the forceps, come out alive, and swim for a week in the vat. On the eighth day a nurse would find him. She'd marvel at his perfect toes and powerful legs, then stick him in her purse and bring him home. At home she'd feed him clam chowder and he'd grow strong. By age four he'd grow a faint mustache. By six he'd start to do little miracles, like turn plain toast into garlic bread. The nurse, who was poor and had once been slutty, would think greedy thoughts at night. Soon she'd ask the boy to do better miracles, like help her and her friends get bigger apartments, and the boy would reprimand her, then explain that he couldn't do real miracles until he became a man and dealt with his mother. After that, he'd say, his work would start. No one was sure what his work was, but everyone agreed that once he started it, the economy would be great. I thought this story was silly. But everyone talked about it all the time and when they did we felt rich, even if we were eating ham and bread.

Now my lover was not looking at me. He'd pulled the compress down over his eyes. I wanted to make it up. I tried to think of a way. But I was too sore for that. And I had a bad feeling he was still angry at me. Unfortunately, there was no time to grieve. That afternoon we had to go to a wedding. I was supposed to buy the present. I was supposed to get it at the mall. But obviously I had not. The wedding was for his best friend.

One sec, I said, as if he were still paying attention to me. Then I got dressed in my red silk frock.

Ready! I said. I thought if I was in a good mood he'd get in one too. Let's go get the present, I said.

Do you really think I feel like going to a wedding? he said. But he followed me out to the car.

We went to the mall, and at the mall we went to Whitman's, our favorite store. It had nice silverware and a very fancy line of coffee makers and dishes, and it was where his best friend had registered. My lover was his best friend's best man, and he'd practiced his toast all week, so he wanted to buy an expensive gift. We walked up to the registron. She wore her black hair in a tight bun, and wore a shiny ebony dress that was tight everywhere except at the ankles, where it poofed into an umbrella skirt. We told her what party we were with and she looked up the list.

We want to buy something expensive, my lover said. It's for my best friend. He took my wallet out of my purse.

I knew it was practically empty so I hummed a little song about how key chains make pretty good gifts.

The registron lifted her glasses. They have signed on for the titanium pepper mill, she said. It is yet unbought. Will that do?

My lover must have looked skeptical, because she said, It prepares fresh pepper at a verbal command, with a choice from among five grades: very coarse, medium coarse, coarse, not coarse, and regular. It was designed in France. It is yet unbought. Will it do?

Oh yes, my lover said.

It is $500, the registron said, and her eyes turned from brown to black.

No problem, my lover said.

He opened my wallet. He found a five-dollar bill and one ten.

He looked at me. Then he looked at the wallet. Where's the money? he said.

What money? I said.

He searched my purse. This morning you had $500, he said.

I smiled a silly smile. But he did not smile back. I turned to the registron. Do you have anything cheaper? I said.

Then my lover started to cry. He'd realized where the money went.

The registron's eyes teared over with pity. What's wrong? she said.

I opened my mouth but didn't speak. I hoped he wouldn't tell her what I'd done.

Nothing, he said.

I sighed in relief. He was going to be discreet.

My near-son died today, he said.

I'm so sorry, the registron said. Her name was Alberta. It said so on her tag. You have Alberta's sympathy, she said. Was he many weeks?

I could see my lover mentally counting. At least twelve, he said.

Terrible, Alberta said. What a loss.

He might have had toes, my lover said.

No toes, I said.

I couldn't help that. I knew I shouldn't have said it. I should have let him grieve. But the thing looked more like cheese than a near-son and I was getting defensive. Plus he'd lied about the twelve weeks. It was more like six or seven.

Toes or no toes, my lover said. He was still my near-son to me.

Who did it? Alberta said. If I may ask.

I looked around the store. I'll just look around the store, I said.

She did it, my lover said.

Oh, no, Alberta said. She looked at me. I'm sorry to hear that.

Yeah well, I said. Me too. Because it hurt like a mother-fucker, I'll tell you that.

I was trying to be funny but no one laughed.

How can you say that? my lover said angrily. You're walking and talking. Think about how it hurt him!

I made a point of checking my watch. It was 2:48. The wedding was at three. I wanted us to get there and to have a good time. I felt bad about the near-son myself. I'm sure if it had grown up it might have been cute. But as I said, we were broke, and I don't like kids. Usually my lover and I got along well. I loved him. When he was employed, he was sweet. And when he became unemployed, I told him I'd support him as long as he needed and that if an analyst was really what he was meant to be, he shouldn't feel pressured to do other work, like wash dishes at a restaurant or paint government tenement houses. And I was keeping that promise. My lover was an analyst and nothing else.

I turned to Alberta. What's your cheapest thing? I said.

The keychain was $14.99 and we couldn't afford the silver-sky gift wrap, but I thought it looked nice in the blue tissue paper that Alberta gave us for free.

My lover perked up on the way to the wedding. He even practiced his speech, and to get back on his good side, every time he read it I clapped. We arrived late, but we saw my lover's best friend and his best friend's fiancée make their vows, and we watched all the parents and relatives cry, and then my lover started crying too and I thought, Oh, no, now he'll blab it to everyone; but he stopped when everyone else stopped, so I figured it was normal wedding crying.

At the dinner I was starving, because I'd been told not to eat for two days before the operation. The buffet was amazing. I put three salmon steaks and two partridges on my plate.

Control yourself, my lover said. So I put one of the partridges on his plate for me to eat later. The place where they had the dinner was the banquet hall of an old church. There were tall stained-glass windows and walls made of huge limestone blocks. The food was delicious, especially the partridges, and even though my lover said he couldn't eat, I hoped it was because he was nervous about his speech. I held his hand under the table, and for a while he let me. Then he shook it off. We were sitting with some people I didn't know. I'd been hoping he'd introduce me, but he didn't. I said something about it and he shrugged. Then he pointed to two people far across the room and said, That's Bobby. That's Joe.

They didn't look up so I just said, Now I know, and ate my fish.

When the forks hit the glasses, my lover stood up.

He walked to the podium, which stood atop a granite platform at the front of the room. Everyone stopped talking. My lover adjusted the microphone. He brushed a hand through his hair. He grinned in the way that showed his teeth and meant he was out of sorts. Benny, he said. That was the groom's name. Benny, how long have we been friends?

There was silence.

I don't know, Benny said.

There was silence again.

Well, a long time, my lover said. And all that time we've been friends.

Benny smiled. This is a good wedding, my lover said. People nodded. My lover said, To your happiness! and everyone drank, and then he said, Many happy returns! and we all drank again. My lover wiped sweat off his nose with a finger.

I've known Benny since I was twelve, he said. We had a group of friends. We were very close. Benny was the first to grab a boob.

People laughed. But I was worried because none of this was part of his speech.

Benny, my lover said. Remember when we were teenagers, and we went hiking in the national park and you pooped on the sacred Indian monuments?

My lover waited, but nobody laughed.

Right then the drugs they'd given me at the clinic wore off. I felt a sharp pain like forks poking my insides. I crossed my legs but it didn't stop. So I made my face normal but under the table I held my hand over my crotch. When I looked back at my lover, he was frowning at me.

Actually, he said. This is not my speech. I've been extemporizing. I had a speech. But I can't give it because something sad happened today.

What happened? Benny said.

My lover's blue eyes narrowed. The thing that happened is sad, he said. If I tell you it'll dampen your wedding.

I was thinking: Crap. Also: Ow. I shoved my fist into my crotch.

Tell me, Benny said. Tell us all.

My lover glanced at me. It's all right, he said. Let's have the next speech.

But we want to hear, Benny said. Throughout the audience were murmurs of agreement.

The forks poked my crotch hard and without thinking I opened my mouth. NEXT SPEECH, I said.

I was sorry as soon as I said it. I looked around like "Who said it?" so someone else might think they had. But people glanced in my direction.

My lover's chin lifted. I had a near-son today, he said.

On a wedding day, someone said.

Yes, my lover said. Then he pointed at me. She did it, he said. All around the room were large circular wooden tables and each one was full of people and all the people at each table glared at me.

My lover leaned toward Benny.

Pssssst, he said.

People leaned forward to listen.

Psssst, my lover said. I wanted to get a good gift. But I had to get you a key chain because she spent the gift money.

Benny frowned. I have a key chain.

I know, my lover said. She spent the gift money.

Oh, Benny said.

My lover adjusted his tie. Actually, he said, in a happier voice, addressing the crowd, I do have a speech, a totally different one I made up at eleven oh five today when I felt the tingle.

My lover looked up. He had nothing in his hands. He must have memorized it. I was impressed because he's not good at memorization. He held his head high and said:

Benny. You are married today. Congratulations. But you should also congratulate me. I had a near-son today.

A few people clapped.

He weighed a pound, my lover said. He was blond, like all the Mintch men. His age was fourteen weeks.

Six weeks, I said quietly. Half an ounce. Looked like cheese. But no one heard.

Eighteen weeks, my lover said, making it up as he went. The surgeons said that, remarkably, he sang a song as he died. If he lived, he would have been a jazz musician. You like jazz music yourself, Benny.

Benny nodded.

What do you say to the death of a musician? my lover said.

I love jazz, Benny said.

Yes, I know, my lover said. But what do you say to a death?

There was silence. Someone said, Boo hiss. Then a lot of other people said it, Boo hiss. The guests at my table pushed their chairs back. I wanted to say, "Why are you standing up?" but I didn't. A minute later the guests at the tables near mine got up and walked off too. The ones who couldn't find seats leaned against the limestone walls.

What do we do, Benny? my lover said. What do we do about this?

At that point I knew that the kiss he'd given me when I'd eaten the second partridge was a real trick kiss. I'd heard about other times like this and none of them were good. But I knew the thing to do was not to seem afraid. I'd heard from the other waitresses at the restaurant that you had a chance of getting forgiven if you pretended to be sorry. I stood up and faced the crowd.

I cleared my throat. What can I do? I said. How can I make it up?

You can't, my lover said. It's too late.

Maybe it's not, I said. I'll go check!

But the exit was far away. And it was a door that led to another room, not to the outside, and some people were standing in front of it.

I felt desperate and said the first thing that came into my head. I guess that I made a mistake, I said. However, I think you should know that in this case, the near-son was very small. It only weighed half an ounce. And even though it was precious to me, it didn't know the alphabet.

No one laughed.

It was smaller than a tonsil, I said.

Boo hiss, someone said. Boo hiss.

And furthermore, I said, a bit mad now, this bit about the tingle is bullstuff. Nothing happened at eleven oh five. That is just way off.

I thought you'd say that, my lover said. In fact, I knew you would. Because I made that part up, about eleven oh five, as a test. So let me guess. Was it one-fifteen?

No, I said.

I didn't think so, he said. Because I didn't feel a tingle then. Was it noon?

No, I said.

He paused. Ow! he said. Ow! He grabbed his own neck and squeezed it, then punched himself in the gut. He was acting out what he thought his near-son must have felt. Ow, ow! he said. Does it look like it hurts?

No one spoke. Then several people said, Yes.

Because you know what I really felt, my lover said, addressing the crowd, was a slow steady tingle all day. And do you know why?

Why? everyone said.

Because, my lover said, today was the day that my near-son was dead!

Everyone cheered then, and I knew that my speech had not been good enough.

You assassinate an assassin, my lover said. And you punch a bully. But what do you do when a near-son is dead?

Quickly I prepared a better speech in my head. I knew that whatever I said had to be full of pathos and had to convince everyone in the room that as a person I had many facets. I thought of my good qualities. There weren't many. Several times in the last month, I had helped an old lady cross the street. But it was the same old lady, she lived nearby. As for my interests, I liked walking through the woods, reading books in the bathtub, and having sex. But everybody liked those things. I knew there must be something momentous about me. But I couldn't think of what it was. So I decided to make something up.

I see auras, I said.

No one paid any attention. Everyone stood up. All the

people who had been seated in the red room and the green room of the church were now in our room, the blue one, and they'd gathered along the walls.

I looked at my lover. I love you, I said.

My lover glanced at me. I love you too, he said. Then he looked back at Benny.

I ask you as a friend, my lover said. As my best friend and a handsome guy. What do we do about this?

The crowd moved forward.

I stretched to my full height, five three.

I'm not sorry, I said.

They were almost to me so I got up on my chair. I'm a waitress, I said. I serve mostly dinners. Sometimes I do breakfast buffet. For the last three years I've paid my lover's rent. I pay the gas bill and sometimes I take him to movies. I do it because he's an analyst, and if I'm not around then who will support him?

Hands yanked my dress.

There's no such thing as a near-son, I said. It's just a story. Please don't touch me. But that was all I got to say.

BIG BEAR, CALIFORNIA

I was miserable that summer. I had chosen to remain at my beautiful school in California because I did not want to return to my parents' beautiful house in Maine. Summer housing was located at the college adjacent to mine, so I moved my few things to a building topped by jutting metal bars as if made from an Erector set. There were only a few, mostly foreign, students on the campus that summer and they had strange courtyard activities of which I was not a part. Six days a week I woke at seven and took a series of buses through Pomona, a city of low, rusted-out cars, pawn shops, and slow-moving faces, all looking somewhere, and arrived at a white mini-mall in Diamond Bar, where I taught three three-hour-long classes, standardized-test preparation, and a thin version of English literature, to a series of Taiwanese tenth graders. They drove to class in their parents' Mercedeses and called me Piggy and Honey and told quick jokes in Taiwanese: I was not fat but they called me Piggy out of affection. They were my friends. At night I took three buses back and arrived at the campus as the foreigners were setting up barbecues in the courtyard and went up to my room, a tiny square on the third floor with a view of what would have been the expanding southern valley if I could have seen so far, if the smog had not covered the valley, and slept. When I was hungry I ate snacks from the snack machine, mostly cakes, chips, and chocolate-nut bars. There was a tiny kitchenette downstairs, but someone had stolen the blender that I had, upon moving in, placed on a counter for communal use, and I no longer liked to go there. On weekends I slept until the weekends were over. In short, I had a very regular life with no one to talk to beyond the children to whom I taught English literature.

When my sister, who had once been with me at the college but was now a lawyer in northern California, called me to say that a friend of hers, Jacob, was living at home for the summer, forty minutes west of Pomona, and would I like to have dinner with him, I said yes.

I am not sure why I said yes. There was a beautiful desert garden, a maze on a hill of rocks and cacti and strange desert flowers, behind a coffee shop, jutting and awkward, like an unfinished log cabin, which was not now open; and I sometimes sat on the benches of this garden, hidden by immense green leaves, while the sun went down, and looked up at Mt. Baldy and its sisters above the colleges. My sister and I, before she had left, had driven up—you could drive up, past the flat foothills and their spreading low houses, into curving roads that twisted around trees and above great fall-aways, past the village of Baldy, where in the winters skiers lodged; daring skiers, because the slopes were only steep crags, really, and each winter many skiers died—you could drive up these roads, slowly was the best our car could do, and reach a high circle, the near top, where you could park and walk around a giant and precarious U that fell deeply down, thousands of feet, into tumblegrass, and had once been an arctic lake. We had driven up there and walked around, saying not much, in the summer, seeing the light gauze of smog setting over the valley below us, and then driven back down together.

Was it like dying?

It was kind of like dying.

JACOB CALLED ME on the telephone, a prelude, and talked to me. I talked to him in my room, on my bed, with the lights mostly out. Or, I did not really talk, I listened, because Jacob talked, about anything: his brothers, his childhood, his talents, which were related to biology laboratories and the viewing of plays; he did not talk of the law, his profession (or profession-to-be; he was, unlike my sister, still in law school). He was a facile talker, moving without warning from one subject to another, and I let him because I wanted him to talk until I was tired.

He asked me, did I like to hike? I did. Had I ever been to Big Bear? I had not. Would I like to go? Certainly. Why not?

It came out later that Big Bear was seventy-five miles away, far east into the foothills of the San Bernardino Mountains; but at that point I had said I would like to go hiking, and Jacob knew of nothing near as pleasing closer. He arrived in a truck on a Wednesday morning (the school was closed on Wednesdays) at eight thirty. He had said eight o'clock; I had said, ten; he had explained that the drive was long and that to get the best of the day we should leave early; we had settled on nine. He was early; but what had I to prepare? I brought a backpack. It had apples. I had bought them at a convenience store close to one of my bus stops. On the drive Jacob talked and I talked. It was pleasant to drive, or to be driven. The land beyond the highway, little mountains, barren of trees, brush grass, rolling, was beautiful, the skin of an animal laid down. The hills grew larger, water ran through the fields, and we arrived at the town of Big Bear. The town was a small beseeching town much like the one in which my parents lived, in Maine—some humble mountains; winding, poorly tarred roads with busted guard rails; a central village of careful sidewalks and gridded boutiques, white-painted frames holding up glass walls.

There was no Big Bear. Big Bear, the mountain, we discovered, was a good ways south. The trails that did exist were subtle, mere widened stretches of shoulder beyond a bridge where a slash of red paint marked a pine. We stopped a local, or what looked like a local, to ask, and he listed several trails. I selected a short one. Jacob had a camera. He asked the local to take our picture. Jacob put his arm around me; I smiled.

THE HIKE WAS not arduous. A winding, cone-lined path, twisting slightly up. Noon hit; we grew hot. We stripped to

T-shirt and tank top. The trees were scattered and the light came through as families, couples with dogs, came rushing down, excited by gravity. We talked of dogs. We talked of couples. Jacob talked of an ex-lover. It hadn't worked; afterward, the woman had said untrue things of Jacob. We'd reached a tumble of boulders, one on top of the other, the size of small houses, and, at his suggestion, climbed up. On top of these we sat and ate the apples and drank a bottle of water he'd brought. The lake, Big Bear, stretched, behind trees, far beneath: a small blue cloth.

Jacob took my picture: me, my arms crossed, on the edge of the rock. I took his; the same. He asked if he could kiss me. I said no. I might have said that I was sorry or did not know him well enough. I should explain that I had known when he'd arrived and stepped out of his truck and put his arms around me that I would never want to make love to him or for him to make love to me or for us to have any sort of physical intimacy at all. Perhaps this was unfair, since I had for so long listened to him tell me about himself on the phone. It may seem my objection was physical, and perhaps it was, in so far as the physical reveals the emotional; what I had not heard in Jacob's voice, a certain angry despair, I had seen in his face. Jacob forgave me, so to speak. He said something along the lines of he understood. We climbed down from the rocks and from the mountain. I thought we might go home. At the bottom we found the car. Jacob drove us around the village and we circled around the lake.

Because we came upon it, and Jacob was taken with it, we rented a rowboat with an outboard. How could I say no?

Jacob rowed. I lay back. I wanted the sun. I wanted to look like a person who spent time in the sun. The lake, after all, was nothing, merely a curve of water around an outcropping of hill; but we could not see the other side, and so we rowed dutifully around to it, remarking on rock formations, a stray parasailer slooping past. Jacob talked, of college and nothing at all, of people he'd met or people he'd known, who might have been said to mistreat him but hadn't known any better than to do what they did; he seemed to be both asking for and receiving advice, and my only obligation in this was to open my eyes, from time to time, and agree.

WE RETURNED the boat. Jacob suggested dinner. I said okay. I wanted to go home, but more than that I wanted dinner. I had not eaten dinner in months. I wanted to choose my food from a list of food.

All of the restaurants were closed. They bore signs in their darkened glass fronts that said dinner at six and back at five thirty for dinner.

It's okay, Jacob said. We can shop. He extended his hand behind him and I took it. Mostly the streets were deserted. A few families wandered in and out of the doors of the shops. The shops were littered with crystal things, bright plastic objects, colorful kites of silk. We touched things, held them up to each other, turning them to read their inscriptions: HAND-CRAFTED, ARTISAN, BIG BEAR. The salespersons remained behind large wooden counters, dark like drinking bars, adjusting small placards and key chains, pretending not to watch. I had the feeling we'd entered a world that did not want us in it. But on the street we had walked together as if we were happy. We had hiked up and down a mountain, a small mountain, a good hill, really, but we had hiked up and down it.

Do you want anything? Jacob said. He was turning a small crystal music box over in his hands.

I did. I wanted everything. Let's go in there, I said. I pointed to a shop across the street with colored flags across its door. We entered and the shop was a cave of rock formations, with delicate items, glass feeders and wrought-iron totems, dangling from the ceiling. The halls extended around colored items in trays into a back room with earthenware pots, Grecian urns, and red garden columns. In the center was a waterfall of miniature proportions, a replica of Big Bear, I supposed, with water spouting from a high rock formation, and on its ledge, two golemesque figurines, their tiny arms raised as if to touch each other.

I glanced at the price tag. It was $500.

Maybe the restaurants are open, Jacob said.

We found one on a high cliff at the edge of the lake. Its back was a wooden deck with round wooden tables. We sat underneath a red sun umbrella and were given checkered place mats by a girl in a gingham apron.

Have wine, Jacob said. Would you like wine?

As we ate, first the deck and then the whole of the restaurant filled with families and other couples. Young girls in cotton sun gowns ran around the deck, elbowing over the wooden rail and staring into the lake below, while their mothers crossed their legs and stirred their drinks with flag-topped glass straws.

I remarked that the sudden crowd seemed strange. Jacob drank his wine. It's the Fourth of July, he said.

How I hadn't known that the day was the Fourth of July I cannot explain except that all I had done was work and sleep that summer and days meant nothing to me beyond being either for work or for sleep.

Our waitress, her yellow hair in a high chignon, appeared with a tray of tortes.

I shook my head.

There'll be fireworks, Jacob said. He placed money by the bill that I had meant to share and then the waitress picked it up and smiled at me.

I HAVE A SURPRISE, Jacob said. I want to show you now.

We exited the restaurant to a sidewalk filled with people and had to zigzag back and forth to follow each other. I asked where the people had come from and Jacob answered that they were like us. They had covered the fields that lined the roads with blankets and lawn chairs, portable radios, cases of beer, white Formica tables, and beach balls, although there was no beach.

I had no good reason to refuse.

The air was thick with the greenness of the lake. It's too hot, I said. We'll be eaten alive by insects. We had reached the truck. Turn around, he said. Spread out your arms. He held up a can of insect repellent. I held out my arms and he sprayed along my arms and chest and down each leg and then he sprayed my back.

Now me, he said.

When I was done he removed a pink wool blanket from the bed of the truck. Underneath were two bottles of wine. We'll have to drink from the bottles, he said. I forgot glasses.

I would have been happy there, by the side of the road, but Jacob wanted to find a better spot, one with grass and where we could lie down, and we followed other trucks, caravan style, along the people-lined roads. One young couple in jeans and gold skin was setting up a portable grill; they waved us over. Children in the van in front of us pushed their noses and cheeks against the glass. Come sit with us! the man called. I wanted to. I wanted whatever awkward conversation would come from the four of us sitting down on a blanket together waiting for the sky to fill with light. The woman smiled and waved. It's too crowded, Jacob said. He drove on until he found a grassy hill. It was not uncrowded. We were not alone. He carried our things from the trunk. In the now near-dark were the outlines of other pairs, restless, getting up and sitting up and lying back down again. It won't be much longer, Jacob said.

I thought of my room, where, I now knew, I had been happy; my ten-by-eight room of ninety-five degrees in the dormitory of gridded iron with only foreigners in the courtyard, entering and exiting in strange-tongued coteries. Lay down with me, Jacob said. It's better like this. I lay back. I could feel the grass and the small hills of ants beneath me.

Do you see the stars? Jacob said. He was drinking from the bottle of wine. There were no stars. The sky was heavy with low invisible clouds, the kind that can't be seen but descend and surround the body.

I'm sorry I'm not much company, I said.

Look. He pointed.

Where?

Above that cloud.

There was a tiny faint star.

Oh, I said.

He lay back. Close your eyes, he said.

I did. His hand closed around my hand. You can see them better this way, he said.

I did not see stars. I planned my own return—my shower, my night, my night clothes, my bed, a book by which I would grow tired.

Those people are kissing. He pointed to an amorphous mass in the dark, moving slowly over itself.

I did not answer. He leaned on his elbows, watching them, without letting go of my hand.

A pale snake wobbled up through the low clouds, flopped down, and divided itself among the clouds above the lake. Others followed, reaching higher, expanding in lemon and ruby and diamond snails. The shapes of the others around us sat up and clapped and howled and we clapped and howled with them. Jacob offered the wine and I drank some. It's good, I said, although it was not—it was sharp and tasted of metal.

Kiss me, he said. Everyone else is kissing.

I'm sorry, I said.

• • •

WHEN WE REACHED my dormitory he did not insist on seeing me inside.

I enjoyed being with you, he said, and I answered something to the same effect. I had realized as we packed our things into the truck that he had drunk both bottles of wine, but said nothing; and though he had none of the signs of an alcoholic, his driving, as we descended the roads that departed the village, was perfectly graceful, as if he had drunk nothing at all.

I fell asleep immediately and did not recall my dreams. The next day I returned to work and the day was long. But I was happier than I had been in some time, because I knew now that I had tried and failed and therefore felt no guilt that I was happiest without the company of others. By eleven that night I lay in my bed, in a nightshirt, almost asleep, reading a book with only the small lamp by my bed lit, ready to be dimmed. I do not know why I had not locked my door except that it was not my habit. When I was almost asleep someone's hand fell against it. I knew that it was Jacob. No one else had a reason to see me at this hour, or, in fact, at any hour at all, unless one of my foreign neighbors needed to borrow something, although I had nothing they would want; in addition, the building was empty. The foreigners were gone for the night, surely bowling or seeing a late-night movie, and that it was not one of them I was even more certain than I otherwise might have been, because of the hesitancy of the knock, as if the knock itself were the request. Jacob's parents' home was forty miles away. I tried to think:

Had he been in the area? What did I leave in his truck? What did I not understand, or forget?

The knock came again.

I said nothing. As quietly as I could, I turned off the light. There would be no answer, there would be no light, and he would leave.

The knob turned slowly, as if not to wake me, and the door opened. He said my name as he entered the room. I had closed my eyes. I hoped it might convince him to leave as he had entered. I saw, through the space between my eyelashes and eyelids, his body standing over mine, next to the bed. He had a shape in his hands, and he stood, not moving.

I turned on the light.

The shape in his hands was a grocery bag.

I thought I would see you, he said.

How did you get in?

The door was propped. He meant the door downstairs. It was always propped. The foreigners propped it, I propped it, the security guards, on their infrequent rounds, propped it.

He placed the bag on the floor next to the clothes I had worn that day.

I brought you things. He looked down and did not smile. He seemed both abashed and pleased. I'm sorry I woke you up, he said.

I wasn't asleep, I said.

I was angry. I was furious. I let it sound, somewhat, in my voice. I was also afraid. I knew the body in my room was a wrecked ship or a ship about to wreck, a tourniquet, a tight wrapping unwrapping, here.

It's okay, I added. I was reading.

He smiled. What were you reading?

I showed him my book. He took it and held it up. I haven't read this, he said. Then he moved his hands inside the grocery bag and withdrew three books.

I brought these for you, he said.

I looked at them. Two of them I had already begun to read and stopped. It was nice of you to come by, I said.

I was thinking of you. He sat down on the floor and smiled and looked around my room, as if, for the first time, content.

I have to work tomorrow. I spoke carefully, gently. I knew he had driven here from forty miles away only to enter my room.

He put his hands back into the grocery bag and took out a container of hard-packed ice cream, the kind that's vanilla with toffee and almonds that I ordinarily would have liked very much.

I know. I thought I would read to you as you fell asleep. I know you go to sleep by reading.

I pulled the covers across myself. He watched me do it. I'm not dressed, I said.

He nodded. I'll go outside. He stepped beyond the door. The door failed to latch and I saw the line of dark from the hall. My room attached by a common area to four other rooms, occupied by three foreign students, now absent, whom I had never met. The common area was dark. A plane moved over the mountains toward the coast. The door opened and Jacob reentered. I'd like to read you something, he said.

No.

No?

I need to go to sleep, I said. I tried to make my voice certain, as with a strange dog that must not hear fear in the stranger's voice.

He stood there. I drove a long way here.

Yes.

He looked around my room. I was ashamed of my room, my mess, my underthings, my food wrappers, my papers and books piled about the floor; but more than ashamed, protective—they were my books, my papers. Nobody had a right to be here.

Let's just talk for fifteen minutes, he said.

Fine, I said.

Okay. He sat down.

Not here.

Where?

Downstairs.

I had the idea we could talk in your room, he repeated, and I would read to you as you fell asleep.

It's a mess.

I don't mind.

I don't want to talk here, I said. My fear entered everywhere in my voice. I want to talk downstairs.

Fine. He was angry. But I have some things to tell you that I don't appreciate.

Okay. I walked downstairs, and he followed. I led us to our lobby, one of those lobbies dressed as a living room, with bare, scratchy, curving couches to discourage sleepers and a

piano and a fireplace to encourage important guests. He sat
across from me on his own Edwardian couch. I sat on mine.
I'd like to read to you, he said, and then he began to read, I
believe, from Alberto Moravia's "The Fetish." It was not, as
the title might indicate, a mythic or sexual perversion, but
the careful nothings of a man, in his room, unable to leave
his room, noting, from his tiny window, counting and mea-
suring the distances and notches of all the buildings within
that block, and then finding a book, a notebook, the writings
of another man in a room, also unable to leave the room, but
a prisoner, who also looked out the window and transcribed
into a notebook the heights and lengths of rusty pinnacles,
water towers, shingles of roofs, corroded mauve corollas.

I thought of my sister. I had followed her here, really,
to California. I had no reason to come, except that she was
here, and because she had begun much earlier than I, she
finished and left, married. I remember standing in the quad
of the college, in a horrible mauve dress, that shimmered for
all the world like a planet. In the pictures I have I am pale,
and next to her, fat, and later, hands filled with flowers I will
hand to her so that she may throw them and I step to avoid. I
thought of her, a lawyer, and married, and married to a lawyer, performing a million trivial tasks with certainty, gener-
osity, and meticulousness.

Do you like it? Jacob held the book in the air above his
thighs.

No, I said. I don't like it.

He placed the book carefully down on the table. You said
you liked to read.

What was it you wanted to tell me? I said. What didn't you appreciate?

Nothing, he said. Forget it. You've disappointed me like everyone else has disappointed me.

I'm sorry it didn't work, I said. I stood up. The furniture in the room—almost none—a one-colored rug and a painting of anyone's landscape, two couches with tightly curving backs—was the furniture of an asylum for the gently, the only mildly, disturbed or aged. He bowed and spread a hand toward the door.

I'll walk you to your room, he said.

When I woke the next morning I unlocked the door that I had carefully locked upon his departure and found the container of ice cream, melted and thick, the cream, though still sweet—I put my finger in—a strange, foamy consistency.

YEARS LATER I was awake late at night. I was doing nothing, alone, late at night, when I saw, beyond my window, down the block, a fire I can only describe as immense, an entire house aflame, and—this was before the sirens had been called and the red trucks filled the road—dozens of shapes, moving slowly back and forth below the houses next to mine, the people who had gone outside to see the fire, which for seconds shot up to the height of the telephone wires and then almost extinguished itself and then shot up again. The neighboring houses, only five feet away, were surely blackening, and all the people on the block, now, it seemed had been drawn outside to see, and I thought: How

morbid, how petty, this unabashed fascination with someone else's tragedy.

I sat in my small second-floor apartment and watched,
by myself, from there. I thought of Jacob. The association—
sentimental, clichéd, or simply unkind; but who can con-
done or forgive an association?—was involuntary. In the fall
of that year I had heard from my sister, who was pregnant
and had taken to mailing me, along with brief notes, small
tins of dried fruits or decorated sachets of herbal tea, things
that she thought I might like. I could barely read her letters,
although they were typed. She was married and a lawyer
and lived in an entire world of lawyers, who played softball
together and together raised vast funds for notable charities
and came together on weekends to teach their tiny and beautiful children to sing, and among all this detail she wrote
well meant things like "It just takes time" and "I know one
day soon you'll find someone" that made me feel as if no
one in the vastness of a million well-named villages would
ever know anyone else. She added, by hand, at the bottom of
one of these letters, that she'd seen Jacob at the law school,
where she'd been invited to preside over the moot court—a
semi-pathetic contraption like a debate team for people done
with high school—and that he seemed well, was scheduled
to graduate in spring in the bottom middle of his class, and
had accepted a job in the Bay Area, where his parents had
moved for their health. Had his skin always been so bad? she
asked. She didn't remember. She wouldn't want me to think
that she didn't think well of me, or that she didn't think I
was beautiful. This was her longest ever P.S. I hadn't heard

from him, myself, after that night, although I had been nervous for a while, when the phone rang, until I realized it wasn't ever going to be him. I'm sure, now, in retrospect, that the fire was set only for the utterly practical purpose of insurance; the house was old, in bad condition, and no one lived in it. But watching, then, I imagined another reason: no reason at all, or anger, or despair; and this filled me with such wonder and sympathy—if I deserved to feel that—for the man of whom it reminded me, and I crossed my arms and pressed my face against the glass.

MONSTERS

THE GROUND WAS MOVING outside the house. First Ellie's plate moved. Then Ellie's sister's plate moved. Ellie stood up. Ellie's sister, Francine, fed her piece of meat loaf to the dog. The dog was happy and ate the meat loaf quickly. Their mother, who was washing dishes at the sink, said, "Sit down, Ellie. Eat your meat loaf." The doors and the windows were moving. Ellie went to the door and opened it. Far below the house, near the lake, three dark trees stood up and became monsters.

"I guess it's monsters," said Ellie's father. He had come outside with Ellie's mother. Ellie's mother crossed her arms.

"Impossible," she said, looking meaningfully at Ellie's father. "They can't be monsters. Those are trees." Then she pulled a large green weed from the flower bed.

The monsters made three dark forms against the lake.

"Those are monsters," Ellie said.

"Trees," Ellie's mother said.

"Wanda," Ellie's father said, "let's admit they're monsters."

"Okay," Ellie's mother said. "But how do you know they're coming here? Maybe they're going next door."

Ellie looked at the house next door. The house next door was not really next door. The other house was a long ways away.

"I think we should go inside," Ellie said. "And I think we should lock all the doors."

"It's a very nice day," Ellie's mother said. "Let's play outside. There'll be plenty of time for locking doors later." She pulled some weeds.

"Can we please go inside?" Ellie said. The monsters were climbing the hill.

"Fine," Ellie's mother said. "If you insist on being pushy." Ellie's family went inside. As soon as Ellie got inside she began locking doors. First she locked the one that led from the cellar into the house. Then she locked the porch door, even though it was only a thin wooden frame and a ripped wire screen. Then she locked the kitchen door. In the kitchen, Ellie's father and mother and sister were doing dishes together. Ellie's father was washing, and Ellie's mother was drying, and Ellie's sister was putting away, even though every minute or so the floor shook and she dropped a dish.

"No one's helping me," Ellie said. "Help!"

"All right," Ellie's father said. "All right." He locked the window above the sink. Ellie looked out the window. The monsters were checking the mailbox. They found three pieces of crappy mail, took them out, and walked toward the house.

"It's too late," Ellie's sister, Francine, said. "I'm hiding. If you weren't so dumb you'd hide too." Francine ran upstairs.

"Maybe it's not," Ellie said. She ran down the long hall toward the front door. But as she put her hand on the lock to lock it, the door swung in. In the doorway stood three monsters. One was very big, one was medium-big, and one was small. They had green and brown fur and where their mouths would be were small black holes.

"Hello," said Ellie's mother, who was standing behind Ellie. "We were just about to hide."

The monsters shrugged and handed her the mail.

"Can I get you something?" Ellie's mother said. "Cookie? Diet cola?"

The mosters nodded.

After serving drinks, Ellie's mother came into the play-room where Ellie had gone to hide. Her face appeared underneath the play table where Ellie was crouched. "You better come out Ellie," she said. "Your sister did. She's being friendly and polite. Why don't you come out and be friendly too?"

Ellie followed her mother to the kitchen, where her sister, Francine, was playing patty-cake with the smallest monster. The big monsters were sitting at the table.

"They only want one of us," Ellie's mother said. "That's not so bad."

"That's sort of bad," Ellie said.

"Don't contradict me," Ellie's mother said.

"Sorry," Ellie said.

"It's okay," Ellie's mother said, "you're forgiven."

"Well," Ellie's father said, "we shouldn't keep them waiting. We should decide." He looked around. "Who should it be? Should it be Ellie?"

"Okay," Ellie's mother said.

"No!" Ellie said. "That's not fair." She looked at Francine, who continued to play patty-cake with the littlest monster.

"All right, Ellie," Ellie's father said, and sighed. "Let's be fair. What's fair?"

"Well," Ellie's mother said. "Ellie didn't eat her lunch."

"Okay," Ellie's father said. He nodded. "Then it should be Ellie. If you think that's fair."

"It's not," Ellie said. "Lunch has nothing to do with monsters."

"Wanda," Ellie's father said, turning to Ellie's mother, "Ellie says lunch has nothing to do with monsters. Do you agree?"

"I don't know," Ellie's mother said. "I've been reading a good book called *The Connection Web* that says that everything is connected. So I don't know if I agree."

"She fed her meat loaf to the dog." Ellie pointed at Francine.

"Oh, Ellie," Ellie's mother said. "I don't like tattletales. How would you like it if your sister tattled on you?"

Ellie squeezed her eyes shut. "Why should it be me? Why not one of you?"

Ellie's father nodded. "Good point, Ellie," he said. "I didn't think of that. But you're right. It should probably be me. I don't mind." He took off his shirt. His belly was large and soft and white.

"I mind!" Ellie's mother frowned, and put her hand on his shoulder. She said softly, "I don't want it to be you. What will I do without you?"

Ellie's father frowned as well. But he put his shirt back on. "What do you want me to do?" he said. "I'm trying to make everyone happy here. If it's not me, then who will it be?"

"Me, I guess." Ellie's mother sat down on the chair. She did not look happy. "If the girls are going to make such a fuss—it can be me."

But the monsters shook their shaggy heads. They didn't really want it to be Ellie's mother.

"No," Ellie's father said. "There's no way I want that. I won't let it be you."

"Okay then," Ellie's mother said. She looked resolved. "Then we have to choose a girl."

"What about the dog?" Ellie said. "Do they like dogs?"

"Shut up," Francine said. "There's no way I'm letting it be the dog. I love the dog."

"True," Ellie's father said. "She's a good dog. She hasn't disobeyed in a long time."

"Plus, I don't think they like dogs," Francine said.

The monsters nodded. They did not like dogs.

"But it's nice that you were willing to sacrifice our dog," Francine said.

"Let's be reasonable," Ellie's father said. "Ellie, what do you consider fair? Is Rock Paper Scissors fair?"

"No," said Ellie, who always lost at Rock Paper Scissors. Ellie tried to think of a game she'd win. Francine won most games of chance, all games of skill, and most games that combined the two.

"Hide and go seek!" Ellie said. Ellie sometimes won at hide and go seek.

Ellie's parents nodded. "Okay," they said. "Okay," Ellie's sister said. She seemed happy. The monsters nodded their heads.

"Hide and Seek," Ellie's father said. "Count to thirty." He pointed to the smallest monster, who covered its eyes with one paw. "Okay girls," Ellie's father said. "You both have to hide in the cellar, and whoever is found first doesn't win."

Both girls ran to the cellar door. Ellie unlocked it, and they ran down the stairs. When they reached the bottom, Ellie's sister stood in the center of the cellar, turning in forlorn circles in front of an old wood-burning stove. Ellie, who had immediately hidden herself extremely well underneath the canvas that covered their father's cracked little dinghy, watched her sister. There was no good spot for Francine to hide. "Five," said the littlest monster. "Four! Three!"

"Get behind the stove," Ellie said. She hoped it didn't lose her the game. But behind the stove wasn't a very good hiding place, anyway.

Francine got behind the stove. The space behind the stove was very narrow and her arm and one of her pink shoes stuck out.

"Two!" said the smallest monster. "One!" Soon the small monster stood in the place where Francine had just been. Ellie ducked deeper underneath the canvas that covered the dinghy. The smallest monster saw Francine's arm and pink shoe and pointed at the stove.

"I see you," the small monster said. "Ha."

Francine came out. "I guess I didn't win," she said. She looked unhappy. The two large monsters appeared on the stairs. Ellie's mother came down with them. The shaggiest one held out a comb. "They'd like to comb your hair first," Ellie's mother said. Francine sat down Indian-style on the floor. The monster made pleasant sounds while it combed Francine's hair. The comb caught and yanked hard several times. "Thank you for combing my hair," Francine said. "I love it."

"Ellie!" Ellie's mother said. "You can come out now. The game's done."

Ellie came out. Francine and the shaggy monster went upstairs holding hands. Ellie watched them go.

"The monsters want to comb your hair," Ellie's mother said.

"No thanks," Ellie said.

"Don't be uncooperative," Ellie's mother said.

Ellie sat down. The largest monster moved forward. Soon the comb caught a snarl and yanked. "Ow!" Ellie said. "Cut it out!" The monster stopped.

"Forget it," Ellie said. "I don't want my hair combed."

The largest monster looked hurt. Its shag ruffled. It walked upstairs with Ellie's mother. A few minutes later, Ellie's mother returned to the top of the stairs. Her hand was on Francine's shoulder. Francine was wearing a large pink ribbon in her hair and she was holding the smallest monster's paw.

"Why doesn't everyone but Ellie go sit in the kitchen," Ellie's mother said. "There's some cookies in the cookie jar for people to snack on."

Everyone went to the kitchen.

"Look Ellie," Ellie's mother said. "Come with me. I'm going to tell you something."

"What?" Ellie said. They had reached the first floor hall. No one was in the kitchen. The monsters, who hadn't felt like eating cookies after all, were playing television tag in the front yard with Francine and Ellie's father and the dog.

"The monsters choose you," Ellie's mother said.

"But I won," Ellie said.

"That's true," Ellie's mother said. "But they like Francine a lot, so they choose you."

"It's not fair," Ellie said.

"Try to be more cooperative," Ellie's mother said. "In the future, try to be pleasant."

"What future?" Ellie said.

"That's all I have to say," Ellie's mother said.

Ellie's father came inside and Ellie's mother went out.

"I don't always agree with your mother," Ellie's father said. "But I do agree to work as a team."

"Dad," Ellie said. "Help!"

Ellie's father pulled a little butter knife out of his pocket. "I love you, Ellie," he said. "I know this knife is small and crappy, but maybe it will help."

Ellie looked at the butter knife. "Do you have something bigger?"

He shrugged. "Bigger wouldn't really be fair, I think. How would you like it if you were eating a sandwich and all of a sudden the sandwich stuck a big crappy knife in you?" He shook his head. "No," he said, "a little crappy knife is all I have. Plus," he continued, "any bigger would be hard to hide in your pants. You should hide this little knife in your pants, and when the time comes, stick it in someone's nose. Maybe that will help."

"Thanks," Ellie said. She put the crappy little knife in her pocket. Her father left and the dog came in.

"Hi, dog," Ellie said.

The dog lifted its nose and licked Ellie's knee.

"I'm sorry I tried to give you to the monsters," Ellie said.

The dog wagged its tail. Ellie put her arms around the dog. The dog wagged its tail harder.

"Don't cry," Francine said. She'd walked in alongside the shaggy monster. She held its paw in her hand. "It's not your fault," Francine said. "I guess some people are born like you. Maybe you'll get another chance to start over somewhere else as a little baby. I hope so. That would be cool."

"Can't it be someone else?" Ellie said. "Can't it be you?"

"No," Francine said. "No one wants it to be me. You better get out there now. They're waiting."

"All right," Ellie said, "all right." She fingered the crappy little knife in her pocket, and then she stepped outside.

KNICK, KNACK, PADDYWHACK

1. TUESDAY MORNING

"This one got nine," he says, dipping his spoon into Blueberry Morning.

"Ten if you count the wife," she says. She has already
read the paper because she gets up first. She likes things in
the traditional way. She does not cook his breakfast, but she
still gets up first, to make his coffee, or to simply see that his
clothes are ironed and correct and to be with him while he
eats the breakfast and reads about the gunmen.

"Did you feed Doctor?"

"Yes," she says, refilling his coffee, "I did."

"Because he's not acting like you fed him. He's acting bad."

"Doctor!" she says. "Kiss kiss!" Doctor comes to her and
she pulls his face.

He shakes his head. "Why can't people learn to use them
responsibly?"

"Honey," she says, locking his briefcase, "don't forget tokens."

He looks at her.

"You asked me to remind you," she says. "You always forget."

"I don't always." He pushes the bowl back.

"And could you also," she says, removing the bowl from the table, "please pick up my cardigan at the cleaners on your way down Ninth? You forgot last week."

"Yes" He takes the briefcase. "Yes, all right."

He is halfway down the driveway when he hears the door open behind him.

"Honey?" she calls. He turns around. "Do you want a PowerBar for the train?" she asks.

"No," he says.

"Okay," she says, brightly, "but yesterday you said you got hungry on the train."

"Oh, all right." He glances at his watch. "I'll take one."

She carries it down the drive, kisses him, says, "Will you be late again tonight?"

"I don't know." He looks at his watch. It is the watch she got him because he was always late for things. "How can I tell you that," he says, "now, in the morning? How can I tell you that now?"

She folds her hands. They are beautiful hands, long and white and thin. She looks down at them. "I only asked because if you are going to be late I am going to the movies with Carrie and William."

"Honey," he says. "Of course you should. Go to the movies with Carrie and William."

She smiles. "Okay. If you really don't mind. I'll leave you a dinner in case you're on time."

2. LOVE

She has brought the hot cloth and the water. He sits up to drink while she washes him. "Honey," she says, "can I have a cute-ster?"

"Yes," he nods. "You can have as many as you want."

"I want one," she tells him. She has the ceiling, the sheet, his body, the stars.

"Okay," he says. "Okay." He takes the towel from her hand. "That's good," he says. "I'm clean now."

3. THE ADOPTION OF A CUTE-STER

He is reading the paper and touching his chin. "Do you think we should get another?" he asks.

"I don't know. What do you think?" He means a gun. He has bought one. She is eating a PowerBar. She has taken to eating them. She does not lift irons or watch her weight, she just enjoys eating PowerBars.

"Probably not," she says. "No, probably not. One works as well as two."

She is polishing the stove. This is affectation on her part since the stove is a self-polishing one. She is swiping the top of the stove with his old T-shirt. "Especially," she adds, "if we're going through with what we agreed on."

They have agreed on adoption. It seems a feasible way, after a generous number of attempts. They agreed, when she pointed it out, that it would cause them pain to have tests to determine who is the cause of the failure. They both suspect it is him.

"What did you put in this coffee, vinegar?" He tilts the cup toward the light. "Have you been cleaning the machine again?"

"I made it like I always make it," she says. "I made it the way you like it. Six scoops."

He peers into the cup, frowns, puts it down on the table. "Doctor!" he says, "Kiss kiss!"

Doctor looks up from yesterday's paper and does not rise.

"Jesus Christ," he says, "the coffee tastes like shit today."

"You're just having a bummer." She gives the stove a satisfactory sweep.

"Doctor!" he says.

Doctor opens one eye.

"He's getting old," she says. One of their years is like ten of ours. They jump around till they're seven or eight, and then their hips turn to dust."

He blinks. "Jesus," he says. "I'm sick of this Marlowe case."

"Why do you take the contingencies, then?" she says, reasonably. She is stroking Doctor's beard.

"It's complicated, honey," he says. "There's a lot of things involved."

"I wish it wasn't so complicated," she says. She pinches Doctor's nose. Doctor whimpers. She told him he would not win the Marlowe case. She tells him whether he will win all his cases and she has always been correct. He stopped asking her some time ago whether he would win. Now he tells her nothing of the details but she knows, anyway, what they are. At night, when she does not want to sleep, she sits downstairs in Doctor's chair and reads the papers in his briefcase. She understands them all. She has taught herself to understand. It came very quickly to her.

"What are you doing with Carrie and William today?" He says their names in a nasal tone.

She shrugs. "How can I know? It's not lunchtime yet."

He limps to the pantry. "Why do you get oatmeal-raisin?" he says. "I hate oatmeal-raisin."

"It was a sale." She hands him a houndstooth jacket. "You asked me to look for sales."

As he is walking down the driveway, her head emerges from the door.

He waits.

"Will you please get my cardigan at the cleaners?"

"Okay," he says, "all right."

"Honey?"

He waits.

"Do you think it's time we get you a new briefcase? You know yours looks a bit doggy now."

"No." He clutches the briefcase. "I don't want a new briefcase. I like my old briefcase. Okay?"

"Yes, honey," she says.

4. LOVE (II)

He opens her twilight gown and finds a nipple.

"What's this?" he says.

She giggles. "It's a brushed-teeth button," she says. "Brushed-teeth like to bite it."

He thinks this over. "I'll be right back," he says. When he comes back from the bathroom, she is clearly asleep, the sheet wrapped around her. "Doll-baby," he whispers. "Pistachio-bottom."

"A cute-ster," she says loudly. "That's what I want."

5. THE WINNING OF THE MARLOWE CASE

He hunches over the paper, his cereal untouched. The flakes, milk-laden, disintegrate among one another. "Four," he laughs. "This one only got four."

"Well," she says, "it's really five, because he got himself in the end."

"Oh." He stares at a spoonful of Honey Squirrel Dreams. She wipes the counter with a fine flax cloth. "William says it's a malaise," she says. "William says we're existing in the crotch of juxtaposition."

He puts down the spoon. Its portion of nuts and flakes splashes onto the floor. Doctor inches, tile-bellied, toward the milk.

"By the way," he says, "you know that William just wants to rub your pussy."

"Oh no, I don't think so," she says, drying the counter with a silk necktie. "William's very intellectual."

He sits and considers this.

"How is the Marlowe case?" She does not look up from the counter, which she is polishing now with a velvet shirt.

"It's going well. Extremely well. In fact," he says, "I'm giving Tracy a raise. She's been extremely helpful to me during this case. I think she deserves a raise."

"That's a wonderful idea," she nods, moving the cereal bowl from underneath his spoon in order to wipe with the velvet rag. "I think you should not only give her a raise, I think you should give her a generous raise."

He looks at her to see whether she is being facetious. "That's what I meant," he says, finally, able to detect no trace of irony in her smooth cheeks and narrow white nose. "I meant a generous raise."

"Oh good," she says.

He clears his throat. "You may get the license in the mail today. I hope you'll be home to receive it." He means hers—she has taken a course—but, though she passed, he hopes that she would misfire, were she to use it. Then the gunman or serial killer—no, rapist—would be momentarily confused, and he, the husband, would use his.

"Oh," she glances at the clock, "I may be home. I may not. The mail comes so early these days."

"Good." He gets up. "I'm glad you'll be home." He limps upstairs and gathers his papers from under the office chair where he has hidden them. He files them carefully into the new briefcase which they have picked out for him. He cannot remember what the special order in which he left the papers was. Are they different, now? He gives up. He contents himself with managing the combination lock—whose combination he always forgets—of the new briefcase in under five minutes.

In the kitchen he goes to the pantry and places four oatmeal-raisin PowerBars in his briefcase. "It may be a long day at the office," he says.

"I know." Her voice is faint, from a distant room. "I know it may be."

"Honey?" He turns back, from the middle of the driveway.

"Yes?" She is there, waiting, in the door, for him to leave.

He cannot think of what he has forgotten. "I'm sorry I forgot your cardigan," he says.

"It's all right." She is beautiful in her day gown. "I only want you to have a good day at the office and do your best on the Marlowe case. If you remember my cardigan"—she shrugs—"that's just an added bonus."

He nods. He decides he will lick her in the night while she sleeps. If only he could win the Marlowe case. He decides to win the Marlowe case. He has decided this before. He's also decided to lose weight. He is not at the end of the driveway before he unlocks the new briefcase, attentively running his hands along the beautiful suede inset, and unwraps a PowerBar.

6. LOVE (III)

"Honey?" she says. He is almost asleep. She bites his ear.

"Sleep time," he says.

"William's writing books," she whispers. "Children's books."

"No," he says, "sleep time."

"They're from a dog's point of view." She tugs the comforter. "He wants to feature Doctor on the cover."

"Doctor?" He opens one eye. "Why?"

"One book is called *People Are Salty*," she says. "The other is *Why Lick Bums?*" She tucks the comforter across her nightgown.

"Jesus," he says.

She closes her eyes. "He's the handsomest dog he knows," she says.

7. THE MISSING LEAF

He is looking in his coffee for a reason why it tastes bad. His cereal sits unsugared beside him next to the morning paper and the new .45.

"Honey," she says, "at the gallery with William and Carrie yesterday I saw a Chinese. It looked very nice. It was lovely."

"Maybe it's time to clean the coffee machine," he says.

She shrugs. "What do you think? A Chinese?"

"I think I'd rather have a Puerto Rican," he says.

"Let's look at everything and see how we feel. Also," she pauses, "Puerto Rican ones get fat when they're bigger, and that's not attractive." She looks at him. Rather than the thirty-eight pant they once bought, they now buy him a forty-four. He is really, he says, a forty-two, but they buy the forty-four because he will certainly gain ten pounds in the winter.

"Terry thinks we're going to win," he says. "Terry thinks it's a sure thing. Terry's seen a lot of cases come and go."

She shrugs. "How do you like your new pants?" Her shoulders move smoothly up and down underneath the blue morning gown.

"They're fine." He struggles to get up and she hands him the cane.

He thumps into the pantry, which is stocked, top to bottom, with oatmeal-raisin PowerBars. They have heard the alteration rumor and thought it best to stock up now, in case the alteration should not be a good one.

"You didn't eat your breakfast," she says, following him into the pantry. She puts a hand on his shoulder. "Are you okay?"

"Fine." He thumps out of the pantry.

"Well," she says, "I'm giving it to Doctor, then."

"Fine," he says. He stands in the doorway, watching the dog move its large rose tongue.

"I hate to waste," she says, "now that the Marlowe case isn't looking so good."

"Fine." He opens the door.

"Honey? Do you have yours with you?"

"Yes," he says. "I do." He is halfway down the walk.

"Check your briefcase." She squeezes the dog's ears. "Check, to be sure." The dog whimpers but does not move away from the bowl of Sugar-Sugar-Oats!

He opens the case and lovingly explores the soft suede interior, filled with his papers, his unworn watch, pain medication, Q-tips, small wrapped chocolates, and a dozen Power-Bars. "It's not here," he says. "Someone must've took it."

"Hold on." She wraps her morning gown around herself. "I'll go look." A minute later she returns, the folds of white silk swinging neatly. "Here," she says. "You forgot it in the study." She gives it to him, nuzzle first.

He looks at the gun. Is it responsible? He points it at the sky. "See that leaf?" he asks. "The red one?"

"Yes," she says. The wind gusts her robe. One black squirrel, caught by that motion, becomes a statue on the lawn. "The red one," she says, "the one with three flat prongs."

He shoots. Two golds and a brown weave down to the sidewalk.

She smiles slowly and claps her white hands. The small applause goes away, down the sidewalk, in the wind. "It was very, very close," she says.

8. THE MALAISE

He is reading the paper. He is especially enjoying an intelligent article by a Japanese writer entitled "The Malaise."

"I see you're enjoying the paper," she says. She is holding Truman, rocking Truman back and forth in her arms. Truman is not a newborn. They could have had a newborn Puerto Rican. But she wanted Truman.

"Twenty-two!" he says. "This one got twenty-two before they got him."

She burps Truman against her shoulder. "It was nice of William and Carrie to renew the subscription for us," she says.

"I guess so," he says. He stares at Truman.

Truman drools.

"Where's Doctor?"

She shrugs. "Probably asleep in his chair. You know his hip gives him pain."

"Doctor!" There is no response. "Doctor!" he yells. He misses the dog. The dog is not gone but he misses it. He does not like Truman.

Truman fists her hair and yanks. A viscous pool runs down her day gown. "Please don't yell," she says. "Not with Truman in the room. It's a bad atmosphere."

"Doctor!" he yells.

"What's upsetting you?" he sits down, pushing Truman's face into her robe. "Is it because you're losing the Marlowe case?"

It is money. She has told him it's not efficient to have a one-man firm. If he had other lawyers, sub-ones, he could take more cases, which the sub-lawyers would solve, producing more money, and he could pay the sub-lawyers less than he pays himself. She does not know what she is talking about. She is not a lawyer. She does not understand the complications of taking on more attorneys in the—his, a, any—firm. The training, the advertising to get more clients, the work involved in getting more clients, enough to keep the sub-lawyers busy. She does not earn zilch. When he tells her this, she points out that she does not lose money, as he is doing with the Marlowe case.

"The Marlowe case is going great," he says. "I'm going to win. Tell William and Carrie not to pluck their turkeys. Tell Carrie and William their horse is necking other horses. Tell those good-fence-neighbors it's just going to be a few weeks now till their cock is kicking the other cocks and I want them to get at least twenty percent."

"You know they don't want that." She shakes her head delicately, watching him attempt to struggle out of his chair, and lays Truman face-down on the table, so that she can give him his cane. "But they would like it sooner rather than later," she says, "if you could settle . . . I've a feeling the other side might settle, if you asked." She hands him his briefcase, along with a snackpack of PowerBars.

He thumps to the door.

"And please pick up my cardigan at the cleaners," she says.

He is halfway down the driveway.

"Honey?" she says.

He turns around. She is also in the driveway, in her day gown. She gestures lightly at the three-pronged leaf, lifts the new bridal revolver, and shoots. The three-pronged red floats slowly down, turning over and over in the light fall breeze.

9. DOCTOR, DOCTOR

"Fatty." Truman smacks the tray. "Fatty."

He is eating his cereal. "Truman," he says, "please give Fatty the paper."

Truman moves toward the bedroom with the paper.

"Truman," he calls, "bring Fatty the paper."

"Truman," Truman yells. "Truman!"

"Honey," she walks in, dressed for the position she has taken at William and Carrie's firm, "I wish you wouldn't be so insistent with Truman. It's emotionally restrictive. Or," she adds, "if you must be restrictive, I wish you'd be better at it."

"Doctor," he calls. His ass lifts awkwardly in his chair. "Doctor!"

"Honey." She frowns. "Doctor's dead."

He moves his head up and down. It seems ridiculous. But he misses the dog. He wishes he didn't. He misses it.

He misses the dog. He misses the dog, dog, dog, dog. Her mother's antique Colonial creaks underneath him. It is too small. His knees hurt. He looks out the window to see if his car has come.

"It's almost here," she says.

"Honey?"

"What?" She does not turn around. She remains, in her apple-colored suit, one hand poised upon the glass.

"Do you think of me when I'm gone?"

She continues to look out the window. She can hear Truman playing in the other room and this brings a smile to her lips. "It may be time to get you a new pair of chinos," she says.

"Yes," he nods, "it probably is. But do you think of me when I'm gone?"

She turns around. "If you were me," she says, "then you would know what I thought."

10. THE LOSING OF THE MARLOWE CASE

The morning after losing the Marlowe case, he wakes feeling strangely well. She is lying asleep, one arm flung up over her head, pulling taut the skin across her ribcage. Her breasts loll neatly toward the left. He knows she has been up all night, secretly and futilely researching appeal possibilities, and he feels satisfaction. He climbs onto her body without waking her. When she feels his front teeth on her nipple she opens one eye and slowly closes it. A blue vein moves in one lid. He pulls her legs apart and kneels on top of her, on his knees, without pain for the first time in years, and licking two fingers for moisture, firmly rubs her outer fold, then her center. Her long white hands, laid down, clench and unclench. He continues. He sees Truman, in his some-bunny suit, standing in the doorway, and he continues, and Truman goes away.

11. HAPPINESS

She is eating her cereal.

"Do you like it?" he says. He has made the coffee, six scoops, and creamed and sugared her cup.

"Oh yes," she says, admiringly. "It's very good." She has read the paper, the Sports section, because she likes to learn new things. The bridal briefcase that they have bought her, quadrangular and black with a little gold handle, sits ready on the table, with several blank papers inside, for note-taking. On the front of the Sports section is a photograph of a man, poised, in the middle of playing a sport. She sips her coffee and studies this. "Sometimes," she says, "I look at other men."

He nods.

"And I realize," she continues, "that those men are not you."

"I know," he says. He refills her coffee and stirs it with a tiny silver spoon. "I know they're not me."

"Well," she says, "shall I see you at five? Shall we see the new movie, the one with the girl?"

"It's not a movie for Truman," he says. "Why don't we see the other movie, the one with dogs. Truman likes dogs." This thought makes him happy—Truman liking dogs!

When she is halfway down the drive she stops.

"Yes?" he asks.

"I'll think of you today," she says. "I'm planning on thinking of you."

"That's fine," he says. "I'll think of you too."

She frowns. "But how will you manage that, with Truman?"

"I don't think as intensely as you do," he says.

"Oh," she says. She considers this. And although she has not often felt this way, she is pleased, and as she makes her way to work, she is almost thrilled.

TWENTY GRAND

ON DECEMBER 13, 1979, when my mother was thirty years old, she lost an old Armenian coin. That winter was cold, and she had been sleeping with my sister and me on a fold-out couch in the living room to save on heat. We lived on a cleared ledge, a natural shelf on a mountain high above a lake. The wind on the shelf was amazing. At night it leaped up to the blinking red light at the tip of the peak behind our house, then skidded back down across the pines and whistled past our windows, somehow inserting, through tiny cracks between the window and the frame, snow that piled, sloped and sparkling, on the sills.

Our driveway was a dirt road that wound through a field. It was often lined by eight-foot banks—which I climbed on my way home from school—with teetering, sand-specked bucket-lumps at their tops. Sporadically, a kid came with a tractor. When he left, the lane was clear. But overnight the wind swept snow across the shelf, up over the banks, and into the road. By morning the drifts were as deep as if the driveway hadn't been plowed at all. Every day, my mother called the kid, who was slow and did the easy jobs in town first, to try to get him to come. Then she shoveled a path to the woodpile and one to the car.

She barely ever looked at the coin. It was silver and heavy. On one side was a man with a craggy profile, a square crown, and one sleepy, thick-lidded eye, and on the other was a woman. The woman was voluptuous, wore a gown, and held something in her outstretched hand—maybe wheat. The coin wasn't a perfect circle, and its surface was pocked. But it had been my mother's mother's, and she kept it in her purse.

On that day she was in a foul mood. My sister was one and a half, and I was six. For weeks, the sky had been a chalky gray that darkened to charcoal in the afternoon. Snowflakes were wafting onto the car. We were going to visit my father. Before we left, my mother glanced in the kitchen mirror, tucked her hair behind her ears, and said, "We're out of groceries. If we don't get some cash from your father, I don't know what we'll eat tonight."

We often drove to visit him. He was a Guard bum for the Air National Guard, and lived sixty miles south, at the base in Portsmouth, where he was on alert. Occasionally, he flew to England to pilot refuelers for the looking-glass planes that swung along the Russian coast, but mostly he was on alert. This was temporary. He and my mother had married young, hastily, out of excitement, and spent five years moving around the country, to wherever my father was posted. But when my mother got pregnant they'd decided they needed a house. He'd switched from active duty to the Guard, and was stationed in New Hampshire. My mother liked Portsmouth. The sea kept the air mild, the streets in the downtown were cobblestoned and lined by brass lanterns, and the university, where she could get a job or take classes, was close by. But the houses there were expensive, and my father's mother, who lived an hour north, offered my parents an acre of land for free. They drove up to the mountain. They walked across the shelf. It was summer. The hay was high, gold and flecked with Queen Anne's lace. My father asked what she thought. He said, "It's just for now;" and she said, "All right." They moved all their things into his mother's house. A week later, my father began to build a bungalow with a steep roof, gingerbread trim, and a small wooden deck, like the ones he'd seen built into hills nearby.

While on alert, my father lived with several hundred other men and wore a pea-green jumpsuit that, aside from the gold-zippered pockets on his calves and hips and the blue patch on his left shoulder, looked not unlike the pajamas that my sister and I wore to bed. The other men also wore the jumpsuits—except for the ones who wore navy polyester suits with stars—and they bunked alongside my father, in a vast facility that, much like a high-tech rabbit warren, existed largely under the earth. The complex was surrounded by two barbed-wire fences. To get inside, we had to stop at an electric gate and be "checked" by friendly black men wearing rifles. Then we walked—I always looked over my shoulder—down a long, dark, sloping concrete tunnel.

In the bunker, we were allowed to go to the library. The room was small, gingery, and hot, with shelves of leather-bound books. On the scratchy red chairs in the narrow aisles lay magazines, their articles about naked women or cars. Brown stuffing sprang out from the seats of the chairs, and cigarettes burned in tins on their arms.

The other place we could go was the rec center, which contained a Foosball table, a pool table (one ball missing, two cues with broken tips), a Parcheesi board, and a soda machine. The cafeteria down the hall smelled foreign and delicious—at its far end were vats of spaghetti and of soupy brown sauce, inside which, I guessed, was steak. Best of all, the food was free. But my mother and my sister and I were not allowed to eat it. We were not supposed to be in the warren, in fact, for more than an hour at a time. But my father sometimes sneaked us into the theater, a room with a few benches and a slide screen, to watch a movie; and when I got hungry, as I always did, he'd carry me into the cafeteria, just far enough so that I could see the vats, then take me back out and ask me what I wanted, so that he could order it himself and slip it to me in the library. Usually I wanted lime Jell-O and garlic bread.

My father was on base five or six days at a stretch, four times a month. He was often on duty at Christmas, and was never sick. He was short and pale. But he had excellent posture. He admired Elvis's style, and Henry Ford's business sense. When my mother burned toast, he told her not to throw it out. He ate it himself and washed it down with burnt coffee from the bottom of the pot. He was cheerful, deeply in love with my mother, and quick to get mad.

However much money he left for us while he was on alert, we were careful with it, spending it until it was gone. Then, on the third or fourth day of his absence, we'd drive to visit him and ask for more.

He'd tried to get a job in town. He'd taken a position at a cement plant, but it had gone bankrupt. Next, he'd signed on with a stationery company. But he didn't love his boss or selling pencils, and soon he rejoined the Guard. The work, he said, was steady. We were all healthy, so could do without benefits. He missed us. But it was neat when he got to fly the jets. The economy would swing up soon. And when it did we'd look at our options.

MY MOTHER ZIPPED US into our snowsuits and dragged us to her Rabbit hatchback. We waited while she started it, swept the snow off, and scraped the ice from the windows. Then we wobbled down our long driveway, the engine ululating through drifts. Once we reached the bottom of the mountain, we drove on sharply twisting two-lane roads, under fifty-foot pines. In the distance were striped mountains, dots of skiers, lifts. After coming down from the Belknap Range, we wound along the last miles of Winnipesaukee. Passing the lake took time, and it was entertaining to imagine the elegant houses that sprawled upon its white edge as our own, and to count the trucks and the bright-colored ice shacks on its surface and predict how soon they'd fall in. After the lake was a long highway bordered by forest, and then the tolls, and beyond them our father.

Each trip was thrilling, because in winter we never left the house, except to go to Tillman's Discount World. We bought nothing, unless my mother saw something we needed. She'd study the item, then touch it and say, "It's all cotton, no polyester. We could use a new comforter. The old one's worn." She'd turn it, see the price, and put it back. Later she'd say, "It's a good deal. It's seventy percent off. It might not be here tomorrow." I'd nod. She'd add, "We don't need it. Your father would be upset." We'd walk the aisles. An hour would pass. She'd buy me a pair of jeans for school. Just as we were about to leave the store, the cart would swerve, go back to home furnishings, and she'd lift the heavy package and say firmly, "The old one has holes."

At home we had great days. She was good at cooking, sewing, and folding laundry. She could wash my sister's diapers then bleach the tub and wash my sister in an hour flat. She did our taxes without a calculator. Sometimes she seemed quiet and marked off days on the calendar. But she also said that our life would be perfect if my father's mother didn't live next door.

My grandmother lived in the only other house on the shelf, a tall white Colonial, and she called often, to tell my mother that once again wind or raccoons had knocked our trash cans over, or to ask when my father would be home. She'd given us land and loved my father, so she also gave advice. If his car was gone for a week, she'd tell my mother that he should work less hard or he'd get sick. If his car was in our driveway for more than two days, she'd call to say that he'd better go back to the base, lest his superiors realize that he wasn't necessary and fire him. In his absence, she sometimes appeared at our door with a gift: raspberry jam she'd canned herself. And, while she drank the coffee my mother had brewed, her eyes would light on whatever was new in our house—a set of dishtowels, a plastic tablecloth— and she would praise the object's beauty and ask how much the object had cost.

That morning, she'd installed a snow fence in our field. My mother thought snow fences were ugly. Also, she had a theory that they caused more drift than they prevented. But three men and two trucks had been in our road at six a.m. By the time my mother heard the drills and ran outside to ask the men what they were doing, her black hair flying in the wind, the fence was already installed. When my mother called my grandmother to say, politely, that she didn't want a snow fence, my grandmother said, "I know you don't, Annah. It's for him." And hung up.

My mother looked at the phone. Put it back on the hook. Looked in the fridge and saw that, except for some leftover meat loaf, we were out of food. She turned to me and said, "She should have asked." I nodded. "Your grandmother," she said, "does not respect our privacy." I nodded again.

But secretly I admired my grandmother, because she read me the books I liked five times in a row upon demand and kept crystal bowls of foil-wrapped chocolates all around her den. She also hugged me a lot, and at times she sat me down for serious talks:

"Your mother spends all your father's money."

"I know."

"I myself waited twenty years to buy a dishwasher."

"I know."

"People should only spend what they have."

"I agree."

"I didn't even think about a washer or a dryer."

"We don't have a dryer."

"Your mother has ruined your father's life."

"I know."

"Want to play Rack-O?"

"Okay."

And later:

"Take this coffee cake to your mother."

"She won't want it."

"Do you want it?"

"Yes."

"Then say it's for you."

"Okay."

WE DROVE the long stretch before the tolls. At the first toll-booth, my mother used the last token in the roll between the seats. She hummed; my sister fell asleep. The snow was falling straight down so that the air seemed both white and light purple and the firs peeked through it from along the side of the road. When the second tollbooth appeared in the distance, my mother's hand moved through her purse. But she kept looking ahead. Then she passed the purse back to me. "Look in here," she said. "See if you can find some quarters."

I looked. I found safety pins, a tissue, and a dinner mint. "No quarters," I said.

She slowed and peered at the tollbooth. "Do me a favor," she said. "Check and see if you find any under the seats."

I climbed past my sister. Her head was on her shoulder, and she had thrush-blobs at the edges of her mouth. I pushed my belly to the hump, and reached into the dark space above each mat. Eventually, I touched a cracker with a soft mauled edge.

"It's okay," my mother said. "It's all right. Come up."

We'd pulled into the toll. My mother looked through the purse herself. Then she told the woman in the booth that she was out of money. That she was sorry, but she could pay the woman on her way back.

"I'm sorry, too," the woman said. "But you can't do that."

The woman was older—sixty, perhaps—her hair gray and short. Above the trim of her parka, her large face was grim, or maybe just red from the cold.

My mother took a picture from her wallet and handed it up. "I'm going to see my husband," she said. "This is him. He's at the base down the road. I can get cash from him as soon as I get there, and I'll come right back." She hesitated. "You can keep the I.D. if you need something to hold," she said.

The woman pointed toward the empty lot to the right of the tolls.

My mother pleaded with the woman, to the extent that she was capable of it, saying we were an hour from home, the roads were bad, she couldn't turn around now, had two kids in tow—but her pleading, more insistent than humble, just made the woman mad. The woman said that if my mother did not pull over she would sound an alarm.

My mother looked down at her lap. Her lips pressed together; she seemed nonplussed. She reached into her purse, unzipped a small pocket, and removed the old coin.

"Here," she said. "It's the same as a dollar."

The woman stuck out her arm, took it, and grunted.

For the rest of the ride, my mother did not speak, and when we arrived at the bunker we did not go in. Instead, we stood outside the fence. I was cold, and I could see Derek, the chief guard inside the gate, waiting to check me. I mentioned this.

"You don't need to be checked," my mother said.

"Yes, I do," I said. "I need to be checked."

Derek smiled at me. His smile said, We have serious business to do. I know we might not be able to do it now. But later, I will check you.

At last my father came out. He was grinning. The electric gate lifted. He ducked under and swung out his arms.

My mother walked into them.

Derek looked away, in order to preserve our dignity—mine and his.

"What's wrong?" my father said.

She shook her head.

We got back into the car and drove past a frozen marsh and some acres of trailers to the guesthouse: a yellow one-story building with a flat tar roof. Its entry consisted of a dining room—a room with a table long enough for several families to eat at—and a kitchenette with a fridge that was always empty except for the perpetually abandoned Chinese food in deteriorating, grease-soaked brown bags. Above the stove were cupboards containing sugar packets, mouse turds, and instant coffee. Down a hall were three bedrooms, each equipped with bed, nightstand, ashtray, clock radio. Typically two or three families made use of the guesthouse at any one time, and the sounds of radio static floated through the hall. In the living room, two brown couches sat atop an orange rug. Behind them was a bin of toys I knew well: plastic rabbits with foolish, ink-smeared faces and stuffed bears with crusty patches on their bodies.

I was dumped in the living room. My mother pulled my father into a bedroom. I turned on the TV and set my sister in front of it. Then I slipped down the hall and sat by the bedroom door.

At first I heard the usual sounds: low voices, metal legs scraping the floor, the radio. Then there was fiscal talk. My mother asked for money. He gave her a ten. She asked for a twenty. He told her ten was all he had, save for a five he'd set aside for himself. She said we needed groceries.

"You got groceries last week," he said.

"We need groceries for this week," she said.

"Here," he said. He gave her the five.

"I don't want it," she said. "What will you use?"

"The food here is free." He paused. "If I want a beer," he added, "I'll borrow a few bucks from the guys."

"You have tokens?"

"Yeah. I have a roll in my car."

A sound escaped her: a sigh.

My knees had fallen asleep. Intriguing Chinese-food smells were coming from the kitchen: another couple had finished their nap and heated some up. I wanted food, and thought they might give me some if I asked, but was too intrigued to leave the door.

"I can't do it," my mother said. "I can't do it anymore."

"Come on, Annah."

"I'm by myself with the girls for a week. Your mother calls every day. I go crazy."

"Why don't you just tell her when I'll be home?"

"It's not her business."

"I don't know what you want me to do."

"You need to get another job."

"We tried that already."

"I need to see you at night. I want you to come home at night like other men."

"I'll apply for shorter shifts."

"That's not enough."

They went back and forth for a while. Truly, I think, he liked his job. He'd never been in a war. Or only twice, and only to fly refuelers for the bombers, which meant he'd hovered beyond missile range and hardly seemed to count. Finally, she said, "I spent my coin."

"Your coin?"

"My mother's coin."

"You spent that coin?"

"Yes."

He said, "I wish you hadn't spent that coin."

"Well, I did."

Nothing. Then, "Why did you do that?"

"I needed money for the toll."

"You said you'd never spend it."

"I told you, I was out of money. I needed money for the toll."

Silence.

"It was my coin," she said.

I knew the coin. I knew that my mother's mother had given it to her just before she died, and that she'd died when my mother was a child. During her life, she'd worked as the superintendent of two apartment buildings in Watertown, Massachusetts, and had owned a corner store. She was heavyset, kept her hair in a bun, and wore a gray wool dress and single strand of pearls, even when collecting rent from tenants or loading coal into a furnace. She had not been home much. But she'd had a lot of friends and had loved her life. In the hospital, she gave my mother the coin and said that it was a dollar, and that if my mother kept it, she would always have a dollar in her purse.

"That coin was very valuable," my father said.

"I know," my mother said. "It was money."

"No, Annah, that coin was worth a lot."

"What do you mean?"

"I mean it was worth a lot."

"How come you didn't tell me?"

"You would have spent it."

Silence. He was right. She would have spent it. Then, "How do you know?"

A long pause. "I got it evaluated."

"How much?"

"Twenty grand," he said.

A cave opened its mouth in my heart. I knew what twenty grand was. I knew what a googol, the largest number in the world, was, too—a hundred zeroes—but twenty grand seemed better. I saw a lifetime of unshared Happy Meals and always getting a soda with dinner at Ye Olde Tavern restaurant. I knew that with twenty grand we couldn't have bought the ocean but it seemed to me that we could have bought Wallace Sands, the beach we went to, and perhaps its section of ocean, and the Isles of Shoals, which my mother was always pointing out and which appeared from the shore as a long humpy gray shadow on the horizon, like a whale.

"You tricked me," she said. I'd heard her sound indignant before, but I'd never heard her sound indignant and justified. "You tricked me," she said again.

"I didn't trick you," my father said. "I just didn't tell you."

She said nothing.

He cleared his throat. "We'll get it back."

"What?"

"We'll get it back."

"How?"

His plan unfolded. It was simple and obvious: The lady would still be at the tollbooth. They'd give her a dollar, or a ten if need be, and get the coin back. A discussion followed. They'd get it back. Then they'd sell it. They would? They really would. Were they partners? They were. Was my father willing to quit the military, sell the house, and move us someplace warmer and more exciting, like Portsmouth? No, he wasn't sure about selling the house. But he thought we could rent it out—maybe some skiers might want it—and use the money to rent a small place in Portsmouth. As for the Guard, he said, he wouldn't mind getting out. The Guard had been good to him. But he didn't want to be a Guard bum forever. He knew guys who'd opened franchises— Kentucky Fried Chickens—and done well. "You just need"—his voice deepened—"seed money and a loan." The bed creaked. If she still wanted to go to school, he said, he was willing to help her look into it.

She said, "I want to decorate it myself. The house."

He said, "I'd like a garage."

"We have to be careful. We don't want to spend it all at once."

He cleared his throat.

"I'd like a new couch," she said.

"You can have that," he said. "I'd like a garage."

"First the move," she said. "Then see what's left."

MY FATHER CHECKED OUT on a one-hour emergency pass. We all got into my mother's car. We drove to the exit of the base, stopping at the gatehouse so that my father could show the pass to the guard. The guard was young, with blond eyebrows and fat hands. He saw us, read the pass, and stopped smiling. He said, "Don't be late, Bill." The gate rose. We headed back the way we'd come.

On the way, I saw a McDonald's. It was in a valley that we could see from the highway, a big gold "M" in the distance. I requested a stop. I mentioned my desire for a Happy Meal.

"We don't have any money," my mother said.

"Yes, you do," I said. "You have ten dollars."

"The ten dollars is not for Happy Meals," she said. "It's for groceries."

I made what I felt was a tragic sound.

"Just wait," she said. "There's crackers in the glove compartment."

"No crackers," I wailed.

She reached back and slapped me.

The slap was weak and barely touched my skin. But I was humiliated, because she was my great love. I vowed that I would never care for her again.

We pulled over just before the tollbooths. We parked in the shameful turnaround lot. My mother and father got out and spoke together near the car. Then they opened my door and studied my sister and me.

"What about them?" my mother said.

My father shrugged. "We'll just be a minute."

She glanced at the tollbooths. Hers was fifth, in a row of ten. Snow-laden trucks were sliding up to the booths at thirty miles an hour, floating on ice and sometimes missing the stop. She held out her palm, and in an instant the flakes falling on it became water.

She said, "We could carry them."

He checked his watch. "Leave them here."

She looked at me, said, "Stay in the car," and shut the door.

I watched them walk to the edge of the highway and grab hands. They stood and waited for several minutes while trucks passed. Then they ran across the first lane, paused on the first toll island, and dashed across again.

LATER THAT NIGHT, I asked my mother what had happened and she said it wasn't my business. But after I asked her a fourth time, she told me.

THE WOMAN WAS still there.

"Sure, I remember you," she said. "You gave me this." She held it up.

Just then a blue sedan slid into the stall. My parents hurried up onto the platform behind the booth, a raised nub, and squished themselves against the booth's metal side. "I have a dollar now," my mother said, when the sedan was gone. "This is my husband." My father said, "Hello, I'm Bill," in his most charming, glad-to-meet-you voice. The woman nodded.

"I came to get my coin back," my mother said. She held out a token.

The woman shook her head. "This coin belongs to me," she said.

"It's my coin," my mother said.

"You gave it to me," the woman said, "and now it's mine. I took it out of the box"—she pointed to a cardboard box on a metal counter—"and I replaced it with my own dollar."

A car veered into the stall. My parents climbed back onto the nub. More cars followed. When they stepped down, my mother had to shout to be heard above the traffic. "I didn't give it to you," she said. "I left it with you for safekeeping."

The woman told my parents to leave. She said she wasn't a fool. She knew the coin was worth money. She could tell, because it looked old. She'd called a friend who knew about coins, and the friend had said it sounded valuable, perhaps very. My mother nodded. Then she begged. The coin was the only thing she had of her mother's, she said, and her mother had died when she was nine. It was why she'd kept it all these years. Yes, it was worth something. But it was sentimental to her. It was her memory, really, of her mother.

My father rubbed his nose. "It's not worth much," he said.

The woman gestured my parents back onto the nub. Then she opened a panel in the booth, and spoke to them through it while she serviced cars. Her own mother was not alive, of course, she said. Her own mother had died years ago. She herself was sixty-two and worked in a tollbooth. She had arthritis and shingles, not to mention other things. She shrugged, and said she was getting it appraised by a dealer, and selling it.

They had been at the booth for half an hour. The sky was dark.

If they didn't leave now, the woman said, she'd call the police.

My mother leaned forward. "It's worth twenty grand," she said.

The woman blinked, and waved my mother away.

·   ·   ·

WHEN THEY GOT BACK to the lot, they found that we were gone. My father was enraged—he was overdue on his emergency pass—but he proposed a plan.

My mother agreed to his plan. She started walking north along the shoulder, looking for us. But then she turned into the woods. She felt sure that wandering into them was something I might have done. It was, but it was equally something she herself might have done. There were an infinite number of places to enter the forest, which stretched darkly, politely, on both sides of the road. It was overwhelming, but also irresistible. My mother was compelled, perhaps, by the hopelessness of the task. Of course, footprints would have been the thing to look for; but the snow was falling thickly and had already left two inches on top of the Rabbit, and she decided that it had covered our tracks. She walked into the forest until she could no longer hear the cars on the highway, and sat down. A tree, a handsome green pine, immediately dropped a load of snow on her head. She brushed it off. Her jeans grew wet. The forest said shuh, shuh, and the pines leaned to and fro in the wind. Thirty more minutes passed; my father strode back and forth by the tollbooths, looking for my mother. He was unable to find her tracks in the dark. He shouted her name and swore a lot. When he finally saw her footprints, he followed them a quarter mile into the woods and found her sitting, covered in snow, under the spruce.

"Get up," he said.

"I can't."

"Get up."

"It's too late," she said. "They're gone. We've lost them, and it's my fault. I never should have left them in the car."

He was a fool, but he was not a fool. He saw that she was pining for the coin.

He slapped her.

"We're looking for the girls," he said.

They trudged back to the car. They opened the choke, pumped the gas, and turned the car on. Then they got out the brush and the scraper and brushed off the snow and scraped off the ice, and got in.

AFTER MY PARENTS had left, I'd unbuckled my sister and pulled her from the car. I'd walked us south along the shoulder toward McDonald's. We'd gone about thirty feet when a white sedan pulled over. The door opened, and a woman in a burgundy coat stepped out. She asked me where our parents were. My sister began to cry. I said they'd gone on an errand, and saw, in the woman's face, that she thought we'd been abandoned. She asked me where my parents' vehicle was; I walked her to it. When she saw the Rabbit—with its mismatched fenders (one orange, one blue) and rusty frame— I saw that she thought they'd left the car behind, too. She squatted down, there in the lot, and brought her large white face close to mine. She asked if I was hungry. I nodded. Her brow wrinkled. She asked if my sister and I had eaten that day at all. We'd had meat loaf right before leaving home. But for some reason when I looked at her long burgundy coat my mouth twitched and I said, "Just crackers."

At McDonald's I ate two boxes of Chicken McNuggets and six containers of sweet-and-sour sauce and drank two orange drinks. My sister was too senseless with sorrow to eat her own, and the woman's husband, Mr. Swendseid, had to walk around the restaurant, bouncing her up and down in his arms. Mrs. Swendseid watched me eat. Then she told me to put on my coat.

By the time my parents reached the police station, Mrs. Swendseid had played three sets of Connect Four with me and was going for a fourth. She'd let me win twice and had won once herself. She'd also described her house on the sea, where, she'd suggested, we might stay temporarily.

I don't know what my parents said when they arrived. Eventually, a sergeant must have shoved a thumb toward the lounge in back.

My father made some stiff gestures toward gratitude at first: "Glad you found them, thanks for bringing them here—"

Which were answered by the Swendseids: "The least we could do . . . on a day like this . . . twenty degrees. That's without the windchill, dear, with the windchill it's twenty below—"

And interrupted by my father: "For Christ's sake!"

Then various accusations came out: "Stole our children . . . we were ten feet away . . . left them alone for five minutes—"

"More like twenty, I'd say. We waited by your Rabbit—"

"You were nowhere in sight. What kind of parent"—this was Mr. Swendseid, in whose arms I was being squeezed—"these babies . . . nothing but crackers for a week—"

At which point the accumulated joy of the two boxes of Chicken McNuggets, six packets of sweet-and-sour sauce, and two orange drinks overcame me, and I threw up in his lap.

"Christ," he said, and shoved me away.

Mrs. Swendseid extended her arms somewhat gingerly. Produced a tissue and wiped my mouth. "The poor dear," she said. "No wonder! No protein in weeks—she can't digest it anymore!"

My father looked very small next to Mr. Swendseid, and, perhaps because of this, was standing far away from him, near the door.

My mother knelt down. Her hair hung in wild curls. Her eyes were dark brown with spots of gold, like stars drowning in a muddy pond.

She said, "Tell the lady you lied."

I took a look at Mrs. Swendseid. Her face expressed disappointment. Her white hair was coiled high on her head; in the press of her maple lips, which she'd colored in my presence, there was a tremor. I saw a snobbish pity in her eyes. I thought of the green train with working lights and three speeds that I'd admired two Christmases running in the Sears catalog, and I had felt I'd get this one from Mrs. Swendseid.

"You're stupid," I told her.

My mother made me apologize. I did. Mrs. Swendseid said that she should have known better than to pick up a strange child from the highway.

ON THE WAY BACK to the base, my parents laughed about the whole fiasco. They did not mention the coin. My father particularly enjoyed the fact that I'd got sick on Mr. Swend-seid, and said more than once, "He was pretty surprised," as if my dinner's ejection had been a swift and patriotic strike in his defense.

But when we reached the base my mother grew quiet. My father got out of the car and walked around to the driver's side.

"Okay," he said.

She looked into the dark. Snow was falling thickly on the windshield, through which the lights along the barbed-wire fence twinkled, exotic and smeared.

"You can't stay here," he said.

She mentioned that she'd hoped he would come home. She said that he could say it was an emergency.

"It's not an emergency," he said.

She put the car in gear. The shift stuck, and she did it a second time.

"Drive slow," he said.

We did. The snow came down in gusts, like ghosts slapping themselves against the car, and I knew we would die. When we reached the bottom of our mountain, it was past midnight. Before the steep hill to our house was a flat stretch of fifty feet. My mother stopped the Rabbit, gunned the engine, and hoped the momentum would take us up. On the fifth try, it did. When she got to our driveway, she pulled hard to the right, the car swung into the drive, and its wheels spun, then spun again.

She got out and got my sister out. "Put your hat and mittens on," she said. The snow had stopped. Around us was the world I knew well: my grandmother's house at the midpoint of the mountain, the road climbing up into the woods, and the little mountain behind, all covered in white. Our driveway was a perfect slide of ice. I took a step and fell. Got up and fell again. I decided to crawl. My mother laughed at me. But after falling a few times she hooked my sister under an arm and crawled, too. When we rounded the bend, I saw our house far ahead—she'd left a lamp on—and the black vigil of trees at the field's edge. At the top of the sky was the moon.

"The moon!" I said. "Ooh!"

It was full. Or almost full, like a lumpy opal or a nice fake pearl.

I howled. The idea had appeal. The forest seemed dark and deadly, the house worse, as if it might be concealing something upstairs that would wait until the lights went out to strike. But as a wolf I was safe. I howled, and my mother howled obligingly, and my sister made a silly woo-woo noise. We heard a weak bark from the trees.

"Hurry up," my mother said.

The yip came again. It was a coyote, the one that skulked by the woods' edge in late afternoon. But I felt a thrill in my loins as when I had to pee. I howled.

"Shut up," my mother said.

We reached the house. She turned on more lights. I saw a maudlin tear in her eye.

"You shut up," I said. I began to imagine that it wasn't too late to find Mrs. Swendseid and tell her I'd changed my mind.

But why did my mother cry? Undoubtedly, for the twenty grand. But also, perhaps, for other things, such as all the things twenty grand could have bought—the house in Portsmouth, the garage, the new job for my father. Or perhaps for her dead mother, the coin, her someday career.

WHEN MY FATHER came home a few days later, he was unusually solicitous for several days. He made dinner and washed the dishes after, and when he drove to the store, he brought back a Hershey's chocolate bar and left it in the china cabinet for my mother, where it disappeared piece by piece. He told her she looked pretty in a blue dress, and in the afternoons he walked to the shed and chopped wood. Then one morning, in the middle of ironing a shirt, my mother paused and said, "I miss my mother's coin," and my father turned from the other room and said, "Then you shouldn't have spent it."

THE WOLF AT THE DOOR

I HAD WORKED LATER than I realized and now the building was empty. I had been preparing some documents; I had a large pile of documents to prepare, one that seemed insurmountable, but just in the last hour I had been making some headway and in my pleasure at that I had forgotten the time. When I realized how late it was I left the main shed, which was dark, and went to the general lobby, where a green emergency light burned. In the lobby was a large, well-lit bathroom, and I went in. Another woman came in and went into a stall several down from mine, and I peed so loud that I guessed she was impressed by the sound, but when I got out she did not seem impressed. "We're not supposed to be in this bathroom," she said. She pointed to a large sign: THIS IS A MILITARY BATHROOM, DISCOURAGED FROM USE FOR ALL BUT THE MILITARY. When she spoke she sounded annoyed, also as if she wanted to warn me, in case I didn't know.

"I know," I said. "It's annoying, isn't it?"

But she didn't say anything else. She washed her hands and left. She was walking quickly when she went out the door, and when I went outside a minute later, I didn't see her anywhere. It was then that I realized how dark it was. As if blankets had been thrown over the tops of the pines, leaving only a faint light on the grass. I ran through the grass toward my house, which was not far from the complex. I ran fast—I took the old dog path over the double stone walls, and then I took it as it continued through the blueberry fields, now overgrown with pine seedlings, the little blueberry plant leaves glowing red at their tips. When I looked to my left, I could see a faint light above the hay that stretched toward the horizon and the road. You could run through the fields at night, and make it, but you'd be lucky. I guessed nothing had come yet because of the light that was left. Perhaps it wasn't time. I didn't think I'd been lucky.

I saw my house—I kept running—it was quite dark. The front of the house was gray and its tall windows were quiet. I had a choice of two doors to run to. The front one was closer, but I didn't have the key. I would have to wait until someone from inside let me in. It crossed my mind that if I knocked they might be in another room, one far off, and wouldn't hear me, or would walk slowly, through carelessness, and wouldn't let me in until too late. The side door was farther off; but I had its keys, but that door had three locks, which I knew would take me a long time to open because I knew I would be clumsy. I veered and ran toward the door at the front of the house. The fields beyond the lawn were utterly gray, the sky above them gray as well. Nothing moved in the grass. But I knew that at the last moment of my looking, that might change; so I looked toward the house, ran across the yard diagonally, jumped up the two huge granite blocks that served as steps, and knocked. I heard steps come toward the door. The door opened. My sister let me in.

I closed the door behind me and tried to lock it but as the bolt was about to push into its hole an enormous body, like that of a wolf, slammed against the outside of the door and the door opened. Outside the door stood a wolf. I tried to push the door closed again. I pushed hard on the door; the wolf pushed hard on the door; I pushed hard on the door, and even though the wolf was bigger than me, I managed to close the door but not to lock it. Before I could, the wolf pushed hard and the bolt slipped out. My sister stood in the hall and watched. "It's not fair," I said.

My body was pressed against the door. By not fair I meant that I had been inside the house, and everyone knows locks are locks and keep doors closed; but this lock was worn down and its bolt was not as long as it should have been. Also, the door itself was badly made and was so narrow that on the side of the hinges a one-inch gap allowed you to see outside. Through the gap I could see the wolf's car in the driveway, so I knew he had driven to the house; he had come with his wife or friend; she stood next to him. She had long dark hair, curly, and she was strong looking, tall, perhaps five ten, and dressed conservatively, in a patterned blouse and suit pants, and her arms were crossed. She would clearly have no patience with us. Meanwhile, I knew I could not hold the door closed long, and the bolt refused to lock. My sister—she was my older sister—stood there and watched me holding the door shut. My younger sister, who is the smallest and youngest of us, had come up behind her and was watching with detached, offhand concern. This did not surprise me.

She was used to having things done for her, has been fed and coddled her whole life, and I did not expect her to take action and help; she was not able to, being so young in her mind, though in her body she was at least eighteen. Meanwhile, the door was pushing inward, and to my older sister, who was still watching the door doubtfully, I shouted, "Get a knife! Go to the kitchen and get a knife!"

She stared at the door.

"Get a knife!" I yelled. "Get a knife!"

Finally she acknowledged me by allowing her gaze to sweep across the hallway.

"What kind of knife?" she said.

"A long knife!" I said. Then I changed my mind. If the directions were too specific, my sister would take forever to find the knife. "Any knife!" I said. "Get a knife! A long knife! But most of all, get a knife!"

She hesitated. She seemed to be thinking about getting a knife. I attributed her reluctance to a desire to minimize losses. She did not want anyone to be taken, but she knew that if they took anyone, it would be me. My sister was gifted with foresight. But only in the short term, and only concerning the ones she loved. She did not want me to die, but she might have steeled herself to the inevitable, because she probably knew that if they took me, they would leave and not come back. Also, she no doubt felt something for the wolves, which I felt myself: they were only doing what they must, and perhaps regretted the necessity—you could not blame them for doing what they had to do. Finally, my sister could hardly help but recognize that it was my fault they were there, through my oversight, my carelessness, through my failure to notice that everyone around me at work had left, while one by one the lightbulbs went out; my sister was disappointed in me, even annoyed. Thus, everyone was determined; my sister to be neutral but helpful while acknowledging circumstance, the wolves to accomplish their mission, me to save myself.

The pressure against my hands was very great. I peered out the crack, which seemed to grow wider as I peered through it. The wolf was standing, pushing the door with one long smooth arm, and he had turned into a man. His friend was a woman; her hair was shoulder length, curly and dark as before, and she had a set, angry look on her face. The man was handsome; he was tall and thin, his face and arms almost hairless, his skin a nice brown color. He was muscular, but not overly so, and had a bit of a baby face, chubby cheeks and a long, straight nose; nonetheless, he was pushing with great determination and was still the wolf he'd been before, hungry and stronger than me. As I realized this the door pushed in.

"Too late," my sister said. "Too late to get the knife."

The wolf shoved his way through the door. To stop him, I grabbed a broomstick and pushed at him with the butt end, but he slipped around the broomstick and stepped into the house and just as I felt despair, my older sister pushed herself at him and the force of her leap carried them both out the door. In that instant, she seemed lost.

The wolf's friend, who was standing in the grass nearby, watched with her arms crossed. My older sister struggled to push the wolf off the step. My younger sister, still inside the house, covered her mouth.

I was shocked that my sister had run outside for me. She had traded her own life for mine. I vowed not to let that be. Even with my cowardliness and my selfishness, which were very great, I could not let the wolf take her life. But perhaps my sister, with her foresight, had known that her life would not be lost; because to my surprise, rather than leaving with her, the wolf was still trying to get inside the house. When I realized this, I pushed him away from the door with the broom handle. I seemed to be successful in doing this. However, the broom handle was now in between my sister and the door, barring her reentry to the house, and the wolf's friend was looking at her speculatively.

I stepped outside and with a great shove of the broom handle, forced the wolf off the step. My sister ran inside. I ran inside and shut the door. I locked the door. The door did not lock.

"It's locked!" I said. "It counts as locked!"

"All right," the wolf said. "It counts as locked."

I could see him standing outside the door with his arms crossed. He became a wolf, then a lion, then gave up and became a man. "But open the door for a second," he said. "We just want to ask you something."

I did not answer.

"Do it!" my older sister said. "It's polite."

I opened the door.

The wolf's friend stood on the top step. Her black hair curled down over her patterned blouse. The wolf waited on the bottom step. "I just want to know," the friend said. "Can we have your phone number so we can leave you a message?"

I hesitated. I did not want to give them my phone number. Mostly because I knew what the message would say—I want to eat you—and I did not want to receive such a message.

"We just want to leave you a message," the wolf's friend said.

"Just give them your number," my sister said. "It's just a message."

After having jumped out the door on my behalf, she seemed exhausted and ready to go to bed.

The wolf's friend took a piece of paper and a pen from her pocket.

"Here," she said. "Use this."

At first, I intended to write my real phone number and even sign my name. I knew it would be courteous to do so. And that moreover, if I wrote a false number, they would be angry when they discovered it was false and would be more determined when they came back. I wrote a false number. I could not bear to write my own. And I did not sign my name. Even if I was out of sight, I felt, my name would focus their attention on me, would make them think of me instead of other people.

The woman with the dark hair took the false number. She seemed satisfied. I felt a surge of victory. I felt like a person who knows how to manipulate the success of her own life.

Later that night, with the door locked and most of the shades drawn, we all went to bed. My older sister and my younger sister went to bed upstairs, where their beds were, and I slept downstairs, in the living room, where mine had been set. When this arrangement began, I can't recall, but for some time I have slept in the living room by myself. I have the feeling this is the way my sisters want it and I understand that want; and anyway, on the first floor, I can watch the windows best.

Before my sister went to bed, I told her about a dream I'd had the previous night. I was feeling lonely and hoped, by telling her about my dream, to convince her to stay downstairs with me for a while. But after she had listened to the tale of my dream—one in which I lived alone, performed a boring job, and led a desolate life—she said, "Your dreams are not interesting. In other circumstances, they might be, but here we deal every day with matters of life and death." I knew she was right. I let her go to bed. I sat in the living room by myself. The windows were dark, the room lit by one dim lamp, and as the wind struck the house, the gray curtains blew back and forth.

SOLICITATION

I WAS WAITING for my lover—I would say boyfriend, but my boyfriend reminds me to say lover, not boyfriend, because we are in school and boyfriend sounds silly for a person in school—and it was late. When my bell rang I thought—here's my lover!—so I opened my top door, and at the base of the stairs, beyond the glass of the foyer, I saw the face of the crack lady, although, of course, I didn't know yet who she was. She was tiny, and her skin was black.

I'm your neighbor, the crack lady called up through the glass, I live next door.

Now I had a neighbor who lived next door, and he was black, and his name was Tim, and I liked Tim very much, so when the crack lady said she lived next door I believed her. I did not want to be rude to a friend of Tim's.

You know Tim? I said.

I'm your neighbor, the crack lady said. I live next door.

So I walked down the stairs and I opened the bottom door, the one that goes outside, and then we were body to body. Hers was strong-looking. It smelled like vinegar.

I need your help, the crack lady said. I need your help real bad.

Yes, I said.

She explained that she needed diapers for her baby, who was out of diapers, and that she needed my help to get the diapers. She said, Sister, I need your help.

I knew we were not sisters. But it was nice of her to say so, and if what she really wanted was crack, I thought, I would force her to have diapers instead by going with her to the store, which was one block away, and which stays open until long after midnight.

The street was crispy and our feet made a fine noise stepping together.

So you know Tim? I asked.

Who's Tim? she said.

Tim is my neighbor next door, I said. Don't you live next door?

I'm new, she said.

At the store we went together to the diaper aisle. Everyone saw us together in the diaper aisle, looking at the diapers. I felt that in some sense this made me her mother. I'm gonna get me some diapers to last awhile, my neighbor said, touching a pack of mega-bonus diapers.

Please don't, I said. I don't have much money. Please get the cheap diapers.

All right, she said. She chose some diapers. These are cheap, she said.

They were not the cheap diapers but we took them to the register.

At the counter the counter boy looked at us funny. I did not think anything was so funny I did not like his funny look.

I need a receipt, my neighbor said.

Do you need a receipt? the counter boy said to me.

That made me angry. He had heard us ask for a receipt.

Yes, I said. We need a receipt. I thought it was something to do with welfare, that if you were on welfare, you had to have receipts.

My neighbor left me outside the store. She took a cigarette butt from the butt-can. I need a cigarette, she said.

Good night, I said. I went to my house. I sat on my couch. I felt alone. By the time my lover rang my bell, I knew I had been fooled.

What's with the diapers? my lover said.

Nothing, I said.

She already brought them back, he said. I stopped at the store to get beer just now. All the clerks are laughing about it. They say you're an idiot.

Well, I said, it's a very crispy night.

I don't like you living on this street, he said. I'll be happy when you live with me, on my street.

The next night I was sitting with my lover. We were watching a movie about basketball. When the bell rang I thought—here she is! But when I looked down from the top door I saw a man at the bottom that I had not seen before.

I went downstairs. Hi, I said.

Is your boyfriend home? he said.

My lover? I said.

Yes, he said. Is he home?

Yes, I said. I went upstairs. He wants to speak with you, I said.

While my lover went down, I sat on the couch and waited. I heard their voices—like trucks on a highway—but I could not hear their words.

My lover came back. What did he say? I said.

He wanted two dollars, my lover said.

Did he want the two bucks for crack? I said.

For milk, my lover corrected. He wanted two dollars for milk.

Oh, I said. Milkman, I said. Then, Do you know him?

No, my lover said. I do not know him. My lover lay back on the couch. He started the movie about basketball that he had stopped before. They know this house, my lover said, and they know you live in it, and I do not like you living on this street. I'll be happy when you live with me, on my street.

Okay, I said.

Now I do live with my lover on my lover's street. It is a very pretty street, much prettier than my old street, and the snow has begun to collect itself so that we'll have a white holiday.

This morning, well noon, that is when we wake up, since we are awake late at night, our doorbell rang. Can you get that? said my lover (who generally likes to answer the door but was naked). I'm naked.

At the door was a man. He was a shaggy man wearing a red wool hat. He looked a lot like the father in *A Time to Kill*—he had eyebrows of wrath and an ivory smile. Got any bottles today? he said.

Sorry, I said. I shut the door.

Who was that? said my lover, pulling on pants.

Bottle man, I said.

Oh, he said. Bottle man.

I stood there.

I opened the door.

The bottle man was down the street, wheeling a shopping cart toward the house of our neighbor.

Hey! I said.

He turned. Got bottles? He rolled toward me.

I carried two cases of bottles from the kitchen and I put them on the porch. Wait, I told the bottle man, who stood on the porch with his cart, there's more.

What are you doing? my lover said.

It's Christmas, I said. It's the holiday. I picked up two more cases and carried them out. I was glad to give him so many boxes of bottles.

Happy crack! I said.

He shrugged. Happy crack to you too, he said.

Inside, I was happy, but my lover, no longer naked, was not happy.

You are weird, my lover said.

Was he a crack man? I said.

No, he said. He's a bottle man.

Oh, I said.

Now I am often confused. Crack man, bottle man, father, neighbor, crack lady, sister, mother, boyfriend, lover, pretty street, crack street, these distinctions are slick and leave their colors on one another, but I have the idea that one day soon my God will speak, and then my headphones may save my life.

THE WITCHES

THE BROADS WERE a blue swath dotted by white sails, an expanse that stretched for miles until at their western edge they were broken by the Forty Islands. So named because there were forty, though many were piles of dirt that stuck up from the water. To exit the Broads and reach the lake's north end, a boat had to go through or around the islands. There were plenty of routes that were pleasant if circuitous. The direct one was a pass filled with rocks. Most of the rocks had jagged tips and stopped just below the surface. But a half dozen in the middle of the channel protruded several feet into the air. These were black and shiny, with globular tops. They didn't really look like witches though; more like women's hunched shoulders and bent heads: six lumpy women who'd risen up out of the lake and were looking, now, back down into it. The stretch was famous for hull damage. But my step-father liked to tack through the narrow often windless hall.

He had a twenty-four-foot yacht. He bought it used, for ten thousand dollars. It had come with an old chart of the lake, a horn you could sound that would be heard for miles, two moldy life jackets, and a bottle of Blue Glo-Clean for the toilet. He taught me to sail when I was twelve. Whether you had a motorboat or a sailboat, he said, you'd get to know the lake pretty well; but if you had a sailboat, you'd get to know it better. Because you would pass through it slower and be more vulnerable to things like other boats, their wakes, and lack of wind. The lake was glacial, deep, and twenty-six miles long. At its bottom were coal barges, several steamships, a railroad car, and an abandoned underwater naval sound laboratory. My stepfather taught me the islands—more than two hundred—whose names and shapes I forgot after getting to college, like Ship and Moose, adjacent, each just big enough for a house, and Rattlesnake, miles long and winding with oak-covered humps. Whenever we anchored off Sleeper, bright green and circular, he leaned forward and said, "That island's for sale. If ten men had three hundred thousand dollars each, they could go in and buy it." He took me with him every weekend, whenever he wasn't working at the garage. My mother didn't like to sail, and was often tired. I didn't have much to do. I had track and my homework, which didn't take long. I was tall for a girl, five eleven, and awkward.

Some days we sailed four hours there and back to Center Harbor to get an ice cream at the docks. Fortnights we entered the races our yacht club held. By fifteen I knew every public landing, pump station, and anchor spot, the names of the other crafts in our mooring field, and the dour expression of each old man who spent the week sitting, pale legs forked and pointing toward the path to the dinghies, in chairs on the clubhouse deck.

After we'd left the mooring field and made the point, my stepfather would stand erect. He'd say, "Where'd you like to go?" I'd say, "I don't care." He'd shut the motor off and ask me to get out the jib. I'd go into the cabin, drag the sail bag from the hold, and lug it onto the deck. He'd be standing in the same position, but his hand would have gone into his pocket. He'd say, "How about the Weirs?" I'd say, "All right." He'd say, "Great!" Open the sail bag, wrestle the jib from it, and add, "Why don't we take the Witches? It's a shortcut."

When we entered the pass the birds on the spars would swivel their necks and a few would lift their long wings and their white bodies would raise and puff as if about to shit. I held the tiller and my stepfather stood atop the head, tightening the winch or staring forward. You had to stay an exact course between spars—just so far right of this and this far left of that. I was always convinced, as the rocks neared, that we'd scrape one and our keel would chip or break off entirely. Instead we'd pass into the bay, where there was a beach and a yellow cliff that held up a boardwalk with a penny arcade, a tattoo parlor, a souvenir shop with fake Indian jewelry in front and pipes in back, and La Cucaracha, a Mexican restaurant.

When I was fifteen or so my stepfather and my mother began to fight a lot, mostly about money. The boat was expensive—its maintenance, fees—and he was always on it. She was tired of being alone. My brothers were four and eight. They wore her out. She wanted to go somewhere tropical. She knew other wives who had and thus she knew which islands were the least developed and where to stay and had brochures. Five nights, a private beach, a cottage. His voice went low. "Maybe next year," he said. "We don't have enough money." Privately he showed me catalogs. Spinnakers. It was why we came in second or third in the races. Our boat was the best in its class, but heavy. The guys with spinnakers had the edge. They cost two or three grand. He showed me the one he'd picked out: green with white stripes. It wasn't the most expensive one in the catalog, he said, because it lacked some technical innovations. But it was high quality. The fabric was light yet durable. On a day with strong wind, it would pick up gusts from the stern the jib missed. He pointed. Far off, in the Broads, was a rainbow-colored spinnaker pulling a boat. He looked down at his feet. "I can't really afford it," he said.

He was right. The checkbook was overdrawn. We needed things, my mother a new winter coat, new curtains, new hand towels and comforters for the beds; my brothers fall windbreakers, guitars and guitar lessons, soccer cleats. To make it up he worked overtime and had side jobs. I wasn't sure how the side jobs occured; I think he sometimes told guys, "Come back after the owner's gone and I'll fix it for this much cash." Maybe he just helped them restore their old cars. At any rate, he'd stay late a few weeks at the garage and come home one night after dark and say, "Austin Healey's done," or "I fixed the clutch on that TR3." My mother would nod. The next night he'd make dinner. Afterwards ask, "Is there anything you'd like that I can get you?" She'd say "Baileys Irish Cream." He'd pick it up at the store and they'd drink it on the couch in the living room and he'd rub her back while they watched TV. But at the month's end they'd meet in the dining room, take the bills out of the china cabinet, and discuss which to pay, and without fail my mother would say, "I think we should sell the boat."

I STARTED SAYING no thanks when my stepfather asked me to sail. He seemed to accept this. When the races came around, he had to ask the other guys if someone would let him on their crew. He'd go down and walk all around the club's lodge and its yard and the guys would say, "No thanks" or "Full." Eventually one guy would say, "All right, Earl, come on."

I spent time on the track. I got a job in the library. A few years passed and I was done. I didn't miss sailing or even the lake. But at the end of high school, on the night of our senior prom, when a girl I'd loved as a child asked me if we could take my stepfather's boat out, because she wanted to go somewhere quiet, where she and her boyfriend could talk, I said, "Why not," and when she asked where we should go, I said, "The Witches."

WE REACHED THE PASS, anchored, and floated off the rocks. I sat on the prow and they sat in the stern. They forgot I was there, or didn't care. The girl's boyfriend was twenty-six but nearly crying. She was telling him that she'd decided to go to college after all, not move into an apartment with him as they'd planned, and he was trying to convince her to stay.

On a lot of nights the lake would have been black. But there was a cloud cover that reflected the lights of the town, and the pines leaning out from the nearby islands were visible. I could see the lumpy shapes bending up from the water off the stern, and in a few the deep crevices like fat women's necks, the grayish lichen climbing on them. Sometimes they seemed to be moving, because they were still and the water was moving, and with it the boat. The movement was a black ball at the end of a string. From time to time I closed my eyes. The air was warm for May, fifty degrees, and through the clouds I could see a few green stars. I was feeling lonely. In my purse were diamond earrings the girl had asked me to hold. Her boyfriend was hunched on the stern's bench, and his elbows were propped on his knees.

I knew that his mother was dead and his father was a drunk. He'd graduated late from high school because he'd been in juvie awhile.

Before that he'd been a soccer star. Now he hunched. But every spring one beautiful girl fell in love with him before leaving him for someone else. His name was Dirk Drew. He was stupid, but he often made good jokes about how stupid he was. He had craggy features, dark curly hair, and worked at the marina, on the docks.

I was there because they'd needed a ride. The girl, Crystal, had a heart-shaped face and green eyes. She'd found me and asked for a ride. I would have sat on the prow for five hours or six. But after two, she put her hand on his knee and said she wanted to go for a swim.

Dirk Drew looked at her. "It's two a.m.," he said.

She took her sweatshirt off.

"The water's freezing," he said.

"I live on the lake," she said. "I've gone swimming in April." She sounded annoyed. She added: "I've gone swimming in March." Stood up and took her T-shirt off. Then she dropped her sweatpants and T-shirt in a pile on the deck. She unhooked the railing and stood in the gap with her arms raised. In the deck lights, her body looked gold.

"There's rocks," I said.

She dove. After a minute, we heard her laugh. She was backstroking. I could see white where her breasts protruded from the water.

"It's warm," she said.

I was surprised by how comfortable she seemed. Meaning she seemed to float effortlessly. But as she'd said, she'd grown up on the lake.

"Come swim," she called up; and she said it to me.

Dirk Drew told her to come back in the boat. He said she was drunk. He said that she'd always regret giving him up and that no one else was ever going to love her like he had. He was drunk. I'd walked to the stern and I could smell his breath.

"Swim then," he said, after a minute. "Ruth and I are going inside."

I knew he wasn't attracted to me. I was too tall. My black hair was rough. My nose was not delicate and I had a square jaw.

He said, "Come on, Ruth," and his hand came out.

She was still swimming, her arms sweeping back elegantly. He was half watching her, too. The boat was drifting among the rocks. I could hear the water washing against them, a kind of music. My stepfather had told me a million times, never to swim between a boat and a dock. Because the water could shift suddenly, by current or wind, and the boat could press its weight against the dock. She wasn't swimming between a boat and a dock, but she was swimming between a boat and a half dozen rocks. I felt a shock of recognition, or misplaced déjà vu, and opened my mouth. I meant to say, "Let's put the ladder down." I thought I had. I looked at Dirk Drew, and expected him to get the ladder from the locker under the bench, and put it down. But I must have said, "All right." Because Dirk Drew nodded and ducked through the cabin door, and once I'd followed, he shut it behind me, locked it, and said, "It's cold tonight."

EARLIER THAT NIGHT, our town had had its prom. It was held in the ski lodge and each year it was a grand affair. There was a catered dinner, photographers, champagne, and a committee of mothers who judged a beauty contest and choreographed a couples' march down a red velvet carpet. Parents attended and observed every event from a balcony over the rafters. Men from the town who were not parents slipped in at midnight and squeezed onto the balcony too. That afternoon, I'd asked my stepfather to stay home. At first he'd seemed surprised at my request.

He'd walked outside to consider it. When he returned he said he'd really like to come. I'd answered that I'd like him not to. He'd repeated that he'd like to, if only for a little while, and then my brothers had been sent outside. My mother had no desire, herself, she said, to go to the prom; she was tired, she didn't feel up for a prom, but she was angry that I'd caused discord over something trivial. My stepfather just kept saying how he wanted to go. How he wanted to take pictures, had been looking forward to it for years, was my stepfather and had paid for my dress. But in the end, he promised not to, if I'd let him take one photograph on the lawn.

I'd put the dress on and been embarrassed. It was tight, shiny, black, and too small. My boobs were practically falling out. The rhinestone necklace—my mother had come to my room and said, "Here, take this, you might as well"— looked cheap. But they'd taken the picture, and wished me good night, and my date and I had left.

Soon after we got there, my date wandered off into the crowd.

I wasn't deeply disappointed, and after he left I danced in the lodge among the crowd as if I weren't alone, until I accidentally stepped on, and tore a small hole in, a woman's long tangerine-colored gown. She made a noise and her boyfriend turned around. I recognized him from my math class, where I'd had a crush on him because he'd been good at math. I apologized to his date. She stared. I offered to pay for the damage. She gathered up the material and studied it sadly. She said, "It's not a question of money."

"Okay," I said. "I'll pay double." As soon as I said it the woman looked satisfied. But her boyfriend did not turn back around. Instead he watched me dance. After a minute he said, "You're the worst dancer I've ever seen."

I moved away as if I hadn't heard, as if my rhythm required it, and looked up at the balcony and saw my stepfather. He was leaning over the railing, peering through the wide pink streamers that had been strung across the beams to give dancers the illusion of privacy. There might have been other people already up there too; I couldn't tell because of the spotlights. But I knew he'd taken off his bathrobe and gotten re-dressed and left the house to come to the prom. He was forty-six. A guy whose idea of a great day was breaking some ones and spending the quarters at the penny arcades. I felt as if I couldn't talk. And I sensed, or guessed, that my stepfather couldn't talk to the other adults on the second floor, either. He had a smile fixed on his face, as if someone had told a joke at his expense. He was standing alone and his head was turning back and forth levelly, as if someone very large were standing behind him and turning it for him. He had on a brand-new red wool sweater.

I went down to the cellar. The cellar was a cavern that ran under the lodge. I knew it well because it was where he'd taken me each fall to buy used skis. There was a bench against one crumbly rock wall. It smelled like earth. There was dirt, in fact, in the fissures in the floor. I sat on the bench and read the plaques on the beams. I studied the old poles, crossed and nailed, of some skiers who'd gone to our school in the seventies and almost made it to the Olympic tryouts. I was listening to the music that came down through the ceiling vents and sort of dancing by myself when Crystal appeared. She didn't act surprised to see me or ask what I was doing down there. She just started dancing with me, and after a while a slow song came on and she reached up—she was only five five—and placed her arms around my shoulders. When the song ended she brought her face near mine and said "Let's leave."

When she explained to me that we should lift my step-father's boat and go out on the lake, I felt confused. She had her own boat—a speedboat. When I asked why she didn't just use it, she blushed and said she'd crashed it waterski-ing the week before. When I asked her why she'd asked me for a ride instead of one of her friends, she looked up and smiled. She had wide lips and a lopsided grin that showed her incisors.

"I feel nostalgic," she said. "I miss you. We haven't hung out in a really long time."

I'D KNOWN HER as a kid, the way everyone knew everyone else. She'd come to my house and we'd spent nights in a blue tent, a plastic one my mother had set up in our backyard. Our house was surrounded by forest, mostly pine and birch because the woods dropped down toward a river—and in the night we'd done stupid kid things. She'd taken her clothes off. We'd been doctors or Indians. She'd lain on her back. I'd said, "I'm going to kiss your nipples." She'd said, "Okay." I'd done it, kissed each nipple twice. I'd kissed her belly button. Then I'd felt strange and stopped. Neither one of us had said anything.

REBECCA CURTIS • 214

She said, "It felt weird."

I said, "I know."

She sat up.

I was afraid because I sensed she'd grow disgusted by me. I thought it was going to happen right then. But in that moment she sat up, on my pink sleeping bag with the dwarves on it, and said, "Now me."

IN HIGH SCHOOL, she sat with me on test days. When her friends asked her why she had, she said she did it so she could copy my answers. She wasn't a good cheater—she copied every answer I chose. I wasn't a good test taker, either. No matter how much I studied, I always made some mistakes. So at the last minute, I had to slip my paper away and change several right answers to wrong ones, so our tests wouldn't match and she wouldn't get caught.

WE DIDN'T LEAVE the lodge right away. Instead we went back upstairs so she could march when they called her name and get her crown. We sat at a corner table with a pink cloth rose in a vase and watched people dance. Guys dancing the limbo in their tuxes even though there was no limbo bar, and girls floating in bulbous gowns. And after a while, she said happily, "There's your stepfather."

He was thirty feet above us, across the room on the oppo-site side of the railing now, and he'd taken the red sweater off. Underneath it, he had on a blue-and-white-striped shirt.

I saw the shapes of other adults around him pushing close to share his spot, and that he was preventing them by holding his elbows out wide at his sides. He was clutching the sweater, his camera, and a glass of the fake champagne they'd been serving downstairs. When he saw us looking up at him, he frowned. Crystal waved. He waved back, a small wave. Then he disappeared.

Crystal frowned. "Why didn't you wave?" she said.

I didn't answer.

She leaned forward. "You're being childish," she said.

Her gown was shiny purple, her bust was a V of black lace. Her dark blond hair was twisted into a gleaming sculpture. She frowned. On her smooth white forehead, two horizontal wrinkles formed. "My parents are here," she said. "They took a million pictures of me. They even danced together on the dance floor." She touched her forehead. "I don't know what your problem with your stepfather is," she said. "But whatever it is, you better get over it. Because soon you'll leave town, and then he'll miss you forever."

ON THE WAY to the yacht club we stopped at her house so she could change, and her boyfriend and I sat in her driveway. The family garage was big enough for four cars; the family house was long and cream and seemed flat, but on the lake side it extended down three stories.

Dirk Drew sighed. His breath was fogging up the car. His huge legs were squeezed under the dash, and he was fiddling with something in his hands: a floatie key ring.

"So," he said. "I've never talked to you."

I nodded.

"You're Ruth," he said. "I'm Dirk Drew."

I nodded again.

He was wearing a blue sweatshirt with a long horizontal rip at nipple-height.

I said: "What's with the hole?"

He paused to think. "Sometimes when I'm waiting for Crystal at the high school," he said, "I steal from the lobby."

I waited. He looked down at the hole. He plucked it modestly.

"It's a field-hockey sweatshirt," he said. "I had to rip out the field-hockey stick part."

"Oh," I said.

"Hey," he said. "What are you doing after you graduate?"

I was going to college.

"I don't know," I said.

"Well," he said, "I'm starting a business."

"What kind of business?" I said.

He leaned across the parking brake. "A taxi service for the lake. It's a great idea. Lots of people who live on the islands or, you know, have summer homes, they need rides sometimes to get groceries when they're too drunk to drive boats. And there's no taxi service. A guy with a boat, who started a taxi service, would make loads of money. And me and my business partner, we're going to need a secretary."

Everyone who lived on the lake had two or three boats. I knew they didn't need rides. They didn't need anything. I knew that the taxi service was a bad idea. But I could feel his enthusiasm.

"Crystal's not really interested," he said. "She doesn't have secretarial skills." He examined the floatie. He squeezed it. "You're pretty," he said.

I didn't answer.

"Oh yes you are," he said. "I've seen you around, and you're kind of big, I mean tall, not fat, and you have nice eyes. Anyway"—he touched my arm—"you'd just have to answer the phone when someone needs a ride."

Just then Crystal got in the backseat of the car, and said she'd forgotten to take her earrings off and thrust up two diamonds. "Ruth," she said. "Take these and put them in your purse."

WHEN WE STOPPED at my house so I could change, my step-father was sitting at the kitchen table in the dark. I walked past him and went upstairs. When I came back down, he was still at the table in the dark. He asked me how my night had been. I didn't answer. "You know," he said quietly, "I didn't mean to go."

He said, while watching his hands, that he'd meant only to go for a drive. And that he'd happened to take the camera with him. He hadn't known where he was going. But he'd happened to end up at the lodge. I'd looked so beautiful, he said. He'd enjoyed seeing me in my dress. And—he said this angrily—there were lots of other parents there, so what was the big deal?

I stepped outside. A second later he appeared in the door frame. His hands were limp at his sides. He said, "I got some good pictures." When I was almost at the car, he yelled, "I had a great time!"

I DROVE to the marina fast. We hit 120 on the straightaway by the airport and Dirk Drew clutched the handle on the ceiling meant for dry cleaning and asked where I learned to drive, was it China, and when we pulled into the dirt lot gravel flew up and cracked the glass and Crystal said, "Where should we go?" and I said, "The Witches."

And then we sat there for two hours while little by little Crystal let Dirk Drew know that she was going to college, and he asked if he could come with her and sort of secretly stay in her dorm room, and she stood up and said she wanted to go for a swim, and I knew what would happen.

But the air was fifty-five degrees, and the clouds were refracting the lights of the town even into the pass, and we leaned over and saw her floating on her back, the current carrying her hair toward the rock behind her, and Dirk Drew said, "I'm going in," and I guessed he loved her and always would. He went into the cabin—hunkered to fit through the door—and I stayed at the side of the boat, and she looked up and gestured at the door and said, "Go ahead, don't be an idiot."

He was on the couch smoking a cigarette. He put it out in the sink when I came in. His mouth tasted like smoke; he put his hands around my back.

"It's a nice boat," he whispered. "But it's no good for the taxi service."

I said, "We should put the ladder down." I felt sad. That is, I had the impression I did. But in retrospect maybe I didn't feel sad at all. Because also I remember noting the feeling and trying to memorize it. After I spoke, his eyes widened and he said, "We should." Then I took my T-shirt off and he forgot.

I DID FEEL ODD on the lake—I felt close to my mother because she wasn't there. When I was a kid she'd suffered periods of melancholy, punctuated by episodes in which she smashed platters on the floor and then crawled among the pieces and said explanatorily, "If it weren't for you I could have had a career."

I'd come home from track and she'd be lying on the couch in the living room. I'd clean up the living room and make dinner. I only made what she would have made: boiled brussels sprouts, baked Tater Tots, and fried hamburgers. My stepfather would come home from the garage and say, "Wow! You made dinner!" and when we sat down to eat he'd say, "This is delicious. You're a very good cook."

After dinner, he'd say to her, "Would you like to go sailing?" and she'd say, "No thank you." After a bit he'd say, "What about a little drive?" and she'd say, "Maybe in a little while," and fall asleep.

We drove down to the yacht club where, because his grandfather had, he had a mooring. I'd watch him study the other men—old ones with wide Anglo faces and blotched red cheeks, fat middle-aged ones and their sons—sitting on the long white deck of the clubhouse. I'd watch him mentally decide whose dinghy he should ask to borrow. I'd watch the men glance at each other while he thought. He'd ask the guy he'd asked the least recently, or the one who'd been nicest to him the week before. Usually the man would say, "No Earl, I'd rather you not." On a good day the man would say: "I suppose so, Earl." Or just: "Bring it back when you're done." We'd walk over to the dinghy and row it out. We'd go out on the lake, and he'd tell me awkward stories about when he was an awkward kid.

WE WERE LYING in the V berth when we heard the crunch. I was half-dreaming. The crunch was a sound like metal on rock; there was also a ringing sound, like a telephone from another house.

Dirk Drew's head went up. He got up, walked to the cabin door, and fumbled with the lock. Eventually I got up and unlocked it for him. Then he walked onto the deck, got the ladder out from the locker under the bench, and hooked it over the boat's side.

When I came out of the cabin, he was climbing back up with Crystal over his shoulder. He staggered onto the deck, lowered her into the stern, and helped her to sit down on the bench. Then, while holding her torso upright with one hand, he pulled her wet hair out of her face for her, and draped it over the seat back. He let go; she grinned and fell onto her own lap. After that, he held her against the seat so she wouldn't fall down.

He said her name lovingly and peered into her eyes. But as soon as he took his hand off her forehead, her mouth opened up and blood leaked out.

I knew I wasn't extremely intelligent. But I felt smart then. Her body was purple and her eyes were wide open. She looked lovely, except for the bruised half of her face where her skull had been crushed.

"She's dead," I said.

"Shut up," he said. "You're not a doctor."

He said we should do CPR. He pulled her off the bench and onto the floor, drew her head into his lap, and breathed into her mouth. He waited, gasped a bit, tipped her head back, and blew in again. When he realized that I was just watching, he told me to sit on her legs and shove my fists into her stomach every ten seconds. We did CPR like that for ten minutes. Afterward, he looked up and said, "What am I going to do?" I didn't answer. I was thinking I'd been wrong about his loving her forever. Because what he'd kept saying, between breaths, was, "They're going to send me to jail. They're going to send me to jail."

I stood up and wiped my hands on a towel. "What about me?" I said.

He let her head go. It landed on the deck with a thud. "They won't do anything to you," he said. "You're a girl."

SINCE HE'D BEEN in juvie already, he was given ten years. My stepfather said he didn't think that made much sense. Accidents happened all the time on the lake, he said. It was a shame that Dirk Drew, a not-bad kid, was going to get his life taken away. He didn't understand how these things worked. But he guessed that Crystal's parents were behind it. They were yacht club members themselves, and that week, for the first time ever, my stepfather was invited to their house for a beer. At their house, they gave him a beer and asked how he was. He said he was terribly sorry. They thanked him for the sentiment. They mentioned that they'd heard I was leaving town. He nodded. They smiled and said, "That's for the best." They weren't angry, they added, at my stepfather. They knew that he must feel terrible. All they asked was that he sell his boat.

He looked up from the beer. "Now just a minute—" he said.

"Earl," Mr. Williams said. "There are codes, regulations." He covered his mouth, coughed.

"Well, my boat's up to code," my stepfather said.

Mr. Williams looked at my stepfather. "We're not really asking," he said. Then he looked at his watch.

My stepfather paid movers to pull it out of the water. He washed and waxed the hull. For two weeks he went down every night and worked on it. He cleaned the head and the sink and he polished the Bunsen burner and sewed up a few rips in the couch. Only once he came home and said, "But it doesn't make any sense."

My mother stepped behind him and massaged both his shoulders. When she spoke she used the soft voice she used late at night when they were sitting together on the couch. "Earl," she said. "You're not thinking rationally. You're not objective. Try to see the issue from the other side. The boat was going downhill. It was going to need repairs. It was junk."

After a long time he looked at her and his chin lifted. "You're right," he said.

He'd hoped to get two grand but was talked down to six hundred because of the dent. The day he sold it he said, "Well, I'm glad that's done. He was a nice guy. He wanted something his son could bang up and fart around in." He paused. "Those were his words," he said.

LATER THAT WEEK he asked me about the earrings that Crystal had had on the night of the accident. The Williamses had looked through her effects and couldn't find them. Had I seen them?

I shook my head.

"Well," he said. "I doubted you had. The Williamses think Dirk Drew slipped them in his pocket with the idea he could pawn them. Personally, I bet they just fell off."

"They did," I said.

"Okay," he said.

He walked away and then stopped. "I think it's pretty gross," he said. "The whole thing."

THE WEEK I left town, I rode my bike to the garage where my stepfather worked. He was in the shop under the chassis of a Ford, but when I called his name he crawled out and offered me coffee from the office pot. I'd passed through the office and seen the coffee and it was thick and burned, so I said no thanks. After a minute my stepfather said it was good to see me but that he should get back to work.

I said, "I'm sorry about the boat."

"Oh," he said. "Well." He looked out the garage window and said he'd been thinking of selling it anyway. A boat was a lot of work. It took a lot of maintenance. He'd had to go down to the club once a month and use goggles and a snorkel to wax it, in order to really get under the hull, even in April when the water was cold. He felt relieved, he said, not to have to do that anymore. My mother, he said, was also glad. He'd have more time now to help out around the house. She deserved some help. She'd also, he added, been wanting to take some trips. So they were going to do that together. He was looking forward to it. His hands spread low at his sides. He made enough, he said. But maybe not enough for all the things my mother wanted to do. But he was going to work hard. He thought he could save up. He could put aside fifty a month. It might take a while. But he thought maybe at some point in the future he'd get another boat, more a racer, since this had been a cruiser and a racer was lighter and designed for speed.

THE SNO-KONE CART

I WANTED THE Sno-Kone Cart for my niece because besides being her aunt, I am also her godmother. If my sister and her husband died, I would be the mother. I think I would be a good mother to my niece. Every morning I would sing her a song. I would never spank her or call her stupid. I would hug her every fucking day, I would teach her good manners, and I would not let her do it until she was sixteen.

The Sno-Kone Cart costs eighteen dollars and ninety-five cents; this was more than fifty-five percent off, the flyer said, from the regular price of forty-five dollars. I could understand why the regular price was forty-five dollars. The flyer had a picture of the cart and a little girl was pushing it. The wheels were yellow, the sides were red, the plastic looked strong enough to travel over cement, and I knew the profit from the Sno-Kones would repay the cost of the cart.

When I was in school people called me retard. But my parents said I was just slow. I believed that until I read a letter my mother left on her desk that said, I'm sure there is a reason God gave me a retard. I asked my mother why she wrote that. She said it was a joke. Then I asked my sister why my mother wrote that. My sister said, Mom really loves you, but when she has a bad day she wishes you'd have heart failure. But you don't have retard face, and technically, you're not a retard. You're just slow. Then my sister said if I did all her chores for a year I'd get faster, and she was right. My reading improved. I learned to drive. When I turned twenty I got a great job. My parents said they were happy for me but that I would probably never get married, but now I live with Rick and we are the same as married. Rick is sixty but we are the same age at heart, which is something my parents will never understand. Rick is a bus driver. Rick has black-brown hair and takes Vivantum. He loves my skin because it's soft, and he loves everything else about me too. He says I can live with him until something better comes along. I said I would live with him forever and he said that only God knows what's forever and we are not God. He is teaching me higher math. Profit is what I was thinking about when I was reading the flyer. Profit and my niece, who I love so much it hurts my heart.

I never thought about her much when she was one. But one day when she was two my sister put her on the phone and her voice whispered, Hello Aunt Daphine. My heart went boom. Since then I've always thought of her. And I've always wanted to buy her a special gift, and the Sno-Kone Cart would be the gift.

I found eight dollars and ninety-five cents in my purse.

I knew my sister, who is a doctor, and her husband, who is also a doctor, could afford to buy the cart themselves. But I wanted the cart to be from me.

I need ten dollars, I told Rick.

What for? he said.

A Sno-Kone Cart, I said. I showed him the flyer. For Caitlin Bug, I said.

He looked at the flyer. He looked at the yellow wheels and the little blue awning to give shade to the operator and the cash drawer where the money would go.

Jesus Christ, he said.

Rick didn't want to buy it. He said, Babies don't need Sno-Kone Carts. So I told him how even though Caitlin Bug would not know how to sell the Sno-Kones, she would like the bright colors and she would like to eat the Sno-Kones, and how, in time, the cash drawer and the flavor packs would teach her about math, and how if we gave her the cart, she would know we loved her.

Fine, Rick said. All right.

He gave me ten dollars. Right away I called my sister.

I'd like to buy Caitlin Bug a Sno-Kone Cart, I said. Is that okay with you?

Sure, she said. Why wouldn't it be okay?

I'll never go behind your back, I said. I'll always check with you.

Okay, she said.

At the store I saw a warning on the box that said some parts were small and not safe for anyone under eight, but Rick said toys need small parts or else they aren't fun. Then he helped me carry the cart—it came in a huge box—to the register.

Forty-five dollars, the saleslady said.

I told her that the flier said the cart was on sale.

Well, it's not, the saleslady said.

It is, I said.

That's tomorrow, the saleslady said. It's a one-day-only sale.

Rick put down the box. Forget it, he said.

I looked at my watch. The time was almost nine o'clock. All around us the salespeople were laughing and closing their drawers for the night. On a shelf behind the saleslady were other special deals. One box had a baby flying inside a yellow helicopter. All I wanted was the Sno-Kone Cart.

Couldn't we have the sale price now? I said. Since it's almost tomorrow?

The machine won't let me, she said, and she pointed at the register as if to show me what she meant. The next day was Monday and I had to work. While I was at work, I knew, all the Sno-Kone Carts would be bought by people who were not at work.

Rick squeezed my shoulder. Let's go home and do it, he said.

The saleslady's mouth opened. Then she moved her glasses on her nose.

Tell you what, she said. I'll hold the cart for you. I'll write your name on the box and hold it back here. You can come get it tomorrow. Come anytime before we close.

Thanks, I said. Thanks so much—and I watched while

she wrote my name, Daphine, on the box, and put the box next to the helicopter.

THE NEXT DAY after work I drove back to the store. I waited at the desk for my turn but when my turn came, the saleslady was a different lady.

The carts are gone, this saleslady said. The only one left is fucked.

I told the lady how I had come the night before and how my cart was being held for me.

She shook her head. They're all gone, she said. Gone, or fucked.

The lady wrote my name on the box, I said. She put it in that corner. I pointed at the corner.

She looked up. Are you Daphine? she said.

Yes, I said. I am Daphine.

A man came and bought that cart, the saleslady said. He said he was Daphine.

Well he wasn't, I said. I'm Daphine.

Then he snaked you, the saleslady said.

I thought I might cry. Everything seemed complicated. But then I saw the man, the one who took my cart, in my head. He was ugly. He'd taken the bus because he had no car. His babies were at home. The babies ate beans and hot dogs all the time. They were three, four, and five, and had always wanted a Sno-Kone Cart.

Maybe he was poor and ugly, I said. And his babies really wanted the cart.

He bought two, the saleslady said.

I thought this over. Look, I said, why'd you give mine to him? Why didn't you check his I.D. so you could see if he was really Daphine?

The saleslady shrugged. I might've, she said. If I'd known he wasn't Daphine.

I stood there.

Fine, the saleslady said. I'll give you a rain check.

Once I got the rain check I left the store. I looked at every man in the lot to see if they had my cart, but they didn't.

I called my sister when I got home.

I got a rain check, I said.

What are you talking about? she said.

The Sno-Kone Cart, I said.

Oh, she said.

Don't worry, I said. I'm still getting it.

I'm sure Caitlin Bug will like it, my sister said. Won't you, Caitlin Bug?

I heard Caitlin Bug near the phone. More D! she said. More D!

That's sweet, I said.

I can talk in ten minutes, my sister said. I need you to wait on the phone.

What's "D"? I said.

She's hungry, my sister said.

Oh, I said. Then I heard snick, snick, snick.

I guessed my sister called it "D" because her boobs had grown to Ds. My boobs are Cs so I guessed my baby, if I ever had one, would say, More "C." Although I knew I wouldn't have one because when I was sixteen, I messed up and my tubes got thrown away. I was in sixth grade and I was doing it with a guy I liked. He was fifteen and in tenth grade. We did it in my backyard where I thought my parents wouldn't see. A week later my parents said they knew I was doing it. Later, in the hospital, I said I wanted to untie my tubes and my parents said my tubes had holes and that the doctor had to throw them away. I acted stupid and didn't talk to anyone for three days. My sister came to visit me and brought a yellow flower. She gave me the flower. I felt so freaking happy when I looked at it. She said that if she ever had a baby, which she wouldn't because there were already too many babies in the world, we could share. I knew she didn't mean it. But ever since Caitlin Bug said, "Hello, Aunt Daphine," I have loved Caitlin Bug.

Rick says Caitlin Bug will grow up a freak because she is still being nursed even though she is three and has every freaking toy in the world, all piled in boxes because there are so goddamn many, and she cries if she has to drink from a blue sippy cup, not a red one, on a night when she wants a red one. But he doesn't know her very well because he only met her once. He was invited to my sister's house for dinner. It was the first time he'd been allowed to come. During dinner Caitlin Bug was eating butter from the butter dish and Rick said softly, Don't eat butter. Caitlin Bug stood on her chair with the blob on her pinkie, and a finger-mark in the butter where her pinkie had been, and she looked at Rick and she screamed. My sister put down her fork. Then she said, Why did you say that?

Rick said, Say what?

My sister said, You told her not to eat butter.

And Rick said, So what?

And my sister said, Don't say that again.

Rick said, All right. Then his finger shot out and went in the butter and scooped a blob and put it in his mouth. Then his finger did it again. My sister said, Stop doing that, and he said, Stop what? and she said, Out. When we got home Rick said, Fuck her. Let's do it.

I used to go over to my sister's all the time. Now she's busy a lot so I call my sister on the phone because Rick says a phone call is no big deal, and if she doesn't like it she can suck his hose. Sometimes when I call she has to take a nap or do a thing and she tells me to wait. So I had called her to tell her about the rain check and I was waiting and I heard snick, snick, snick. I said, Do you think I'm okay as a godmother?

Sure, my sister said.

I want to be a good godmother, I said.

My sister didn't say anything. Then she said, Actually, you're not the only godmother.

I'm not? I said.

No, she said.

How many are there? I said.

Eight, she said. She listed them. They were her friends, two sisters-in-law, a cousin, her UPS guy, and her therapist.

Well, I said, who would get her if you die?

If I die? my sister said.

You won't, I said. But if you did, which godmother would be in charge?

Not you, my sister said.

Oh, I said.

You don't have experience, my sister said. Plus Caitlin Bug doesn't like you.

Maybe I could babysit some time, I said.

I'd love for you to babysit once she's older, my sister said. When she's seven she'll be used to strangers, and then we'd love to have you babysit.

My sister said, I have to go.

I TOLD RICK we were not the only godmother. I told him that really, we were hardly anything at all. Rick said some mean things about Caitlin Bug and then about babies in general. Then he said, Who cares? I love you very fucking much. You know that, right?

TWELVE WEEKS LATER, a letter came saying my Sno-Kone Cart had arrived. By then I had forgotten about the cart. I had had a bad week at my great job. Some of the other stockers got fired. The manager told the rest of us we better stock fast because they might fire us too so they could hire some high schoolers who would work for minimum, but that they hadn't fired us yet because they needed us to train the high schoolers. I was worried because I needed the job. But I drove to the store and bought the Sno-Kone Cart because I didn't want to get snaked. Also I was excited. I couldn't believe I was getting the cart, and bought ten extra tubes of syrup, just in case she ever ran out. When I got home I put them in the box with the cart and I wrapped the box in Christmas paper. I wrote, To Caitlin Bug, from Daphine, your number Eight Godmother, on a piece of paper, and taped the paper to the box.

I called my sister.

She blew some air in the phone. We need to talk, she said. Then she said she didn't want Caitlin Bug to have the cart. I thought she meant because Caitlin Bug has so many toys. I said, What's one more toy? My sister said she didn't want me to spend my money on Caitlin Bug. I said I wanted to, and if not on Caitlin Bug then who?

Yourself, she said.

I told her I would rather spend it on Caitlin Bug.

You're generous and kind, she said. Then she told me she was taking back my godmotherhood. She said I wasn't the right person for Caitlin Bug to live with if she, her husband, and the seven other godmothers died. I asked why. She said she thought I knew why. I said I did not know. She said she didn't want to hurt my feelings by telling me. I said, Go ahead, tell me.

She said I didn't understand how much baby food and baby doctors cost and also that I was twenty-two and living with Rick, who was sixty.

That has nothing to do with Caitlin Bug, I said.

It does, she said, because he's using you for doing it.

Maybe so, I said, but you're wrong.

Test him, she said.

I'm not testing him, I said.

Do it, she said.

No way, I said. I don't want to.

She said it didn't matter. She said that I wasn't the right choice for godmother, because I was weird and obsessive and practically waiting for her to die so I could have Caitlin Bug, and also that I had big thighs and yellow teeth, which gave Caitlin Bug bad dreams. Couldn't I see that when I came over, I made her cry? I said I had thought that Caitlin Bug was crying because she was sad, and my sister said no, it was me.

Oh, I said.

I'm sorry, my sister said. I did not want to hurt your feelings.

I know, I said.

You're my sister, my sister said. I share seventy-five percent of your genes. Then she said next time I came over I should just not focus on Caitlin Bug and not talk to her, look at her, or go near her.

I said, Good idea, and thank you for the advice. I hung up. I looked at my picture of Caitlin Bug. She had curly red hair, large blue eyes, and was beautiful. I looked in the mirror. I saw a woman who had big thighs. I opened my mouth. I saw yellow teeth. I went in the living room to see Rick. He was watching TV. When he saw me, he turned the TV off. I told Rick, while talking with my mouth shut, about the phone call. He said he was sorry that my sister had been mean. I said she had not been, that she was just doing what was best for Caitlin Bug. He patted my shoulder, and turned on the TV. I thought: I will never, never test him.

Rick, I said. If we could never do it again, would you still want to live with me?

He looked at me and then at the TV. He stared at the TV. He scratched his head. Probably not, he said. Then I felt my heart go squish, squish, like someone had squeezed it twice, and also it felt like my lungs stopped, but I said I understood. I put the cart in the car, and said I might go for a drive. I drove to the part of the town where poor people live where there are a lot of small, crappy parks.

I found a small, crappy park. In the middle of the park was a puddle filled with sewage runoff. Past the puddle was a swing set with two swings. The third had fallen off. I left my car several blocks away so when I was ready, I could leave without being seen. I dragged the box to the middle of the park. I put it next to the puddle. I took off the piece of paper where I'd written "To Caitlin Bug" and I crossed out "Caitlin Bug" and I turned the paper to the blank side and wrote, "Sno-Kone Cart." I went to the edge of the park. I hid behind two trees. I did not move from behind the trees, even when two poor children entered the park. I'd decided I would not come out and explain to them the things you could do with a Sno-Kone Cart, because I did not want them to scream and run away. This worked. The two girls went right to the box.

I put Rick out of my head, and I put my sister out, and I put Caitlin Bug out. I knew I could not be the only person in the world who liked Sno-Kone Carts. I felt a spider in my heart. It was jumping around. It was saying, Open it. Open it. I felt so excited, because I knew how happy the girls were going to be as soon as they opened the box, and I knew that they would love it and would always remember getting it.

ACKNOWLEDGMENTS

Grateful thanks for invaluable support: Sarah Chalfant and Kathryn Lewis, Esther Newberg and Liz Farrell, and for amazing edits, Tim Duggan and Allison Lorentzen, Meghan O'Rourke, Bill Buford, Field Maloney, Deborah Treisman, Ben Metcalf, and Christian Lorentzen; for brilliant readings, edits, and encouragement, Adam Desnoyers, Keith Gessen, Chad Harbach, and Robin Kirman; my classmates at Syracuse and teachers, especially George Saunders, Diane Williams, Robert O'Connor, Brooks Haxton, and Michael Burkhard; and thanks to my family for love and encouragement. I'm also indebted, for their generous support, to the Rona Jaffe and Saltonstall foundations.

About the author

About the book

Insights,
Interviews
& More . . .

Read on

Meet Rebecca Curtis

© Sean Hemmerle

I GREW UP (from the age of two) in Gilford, New Hampshire, a semi-rural town of five thousand people on a small road named after my family. Gilford is part of the Lakes Region, so named for the lakes and mountains. It's a scenic area, and many tourists come from around the country—in summer to go boating, tour around, and swim in the lake; in fall to see the foliage and hike in the mountains; and in winter to ski. Both my sister and I felt, growing up in such a beautiful, rural, isolated, and homogenous area, that we wanted to go somewhere more exciting as soon as we could. Basically we hated it and felt we lived in Hicksville. We both left the area after high school. But when

I wrote the stories in this book, each began with the desire to describe a place in New Hampshire that I knew, even if it was an ugly place. The setting for "The Alpine Slide" is based on a local water park where I worked as a slide attendant, as did a bunch of other teenagers. That was the best job I ever had, working in the valley among the mountains, riding the slide; in writing the story, all I wanted to do was describe the park. Since almost all of the stories in this book are set in New Hampshire, and since I probably did no justice to the places—I thought I'd compile, as an apology, a guide to some truly great highlights of the area. Many of these places are mentioned in the stories. ॐ

Thirteen Ways to Live Free or Die in the Granite State

1. Troll the Boardwalk at the Weirs
   (www.weirsbeach.net)

Cost: Free. Location: Weirs Beach. Lake Winnipesaukee is a glacial lake with 282 miles of shoreline in the foothills of the White Mountains. The Weirs is a historic area, a family vacation spot, and a strip. This is where, when I was a teenager, I went looking to meet guys from Massachusetts who were in town vacationing and had keys to their dads' speedboats. Also where, when my dad was a teenager, he drag raced his souped-up convertibles. The atmosphere is glamorous, the sign above the boulevard large and neon. The promenade stretches six blocks and sits high above a bay; on it, you can play the penny arcades, ride the bumper cars, get a tattoo, eat a cheeseburger at Jean's Diner or a steak in the restaurant at the pier's end. The shops sell turquoise jewelry, beaded leather vests, homemade taffy, and Indian artifacts; one shop is dedicated to do-it-yourself iron-on T-shirts. Below the boardwalk, the beach (free entry by foot) is long, wide, and sandy. From it you can watch boats of all kinds pass into Winnipesaukee (from Winnisquam) through the adjacent stone bridge–covered channel. Fridays at dusk there are fireworks above the bay. The lake's largest cruise ship, the MS *Mount Washington*, docks at the pier, and on Sunday evenings a jazz quartet plays. Within a few blocks are go-karts, mini-golf, two water parks, and a three-screen drive-in theater. A scenic railroad that circles the lake has a station here. Cheap motels are ubiquitous. If you want something nice, stay at the Brickyard Mountain, which has horseback riding. The Weirs also hosts annual events: the Fishing Derby and an antique car show in late May, an outdoor quilting show in August, and Bike Week in mid-June—when one hundred thousand motorcyclists come to the strip, set up tents and barbecues and tables (to sell leather gear) and party. At this time, spectators and biker babes line the strip and show their boobs when passersby yell, "Show your boobs!"

2. Ride the Alpine Slide at Attitash
   (www.attitash.com)

Cost: $15 for a single ride; $15 for a child's day pass, $35 for an adult. The day pass includes use of the Alpine Slides, Aquaboggan Water Park, lift-serviced mountain biking, skate park, EuroBungy Trampoline, and climbing wall. Location: Route 302, Bartlett, New Hampshire. There are a half dozen or so Alpine Slides scattered throughout the United States, and I have a feeling that in ten years, they'll all be gone. Basically, an Alpine Slide is a cement slide that runs from the top to the bottom of a mountain. You ride a gondola up a ski slope, in summer, while chatting with a friend; then you walk along a rocky, tree-shaded ridge while hefting your sled; then you drop it in the track, test your brake, and race your friend down the mountain. Best part? The wind in your face, the terrifying speed, and catching air on the dips. The worst? Having to stop at the bottom. Thirty-five dollars seems high, but for a whole day ▶

> 66 [During Bike Week] spectators and biker babes line the strip and show their boobs when passersby yell, 'Show your boobs!' 99

5

**Thirteen Ways to Live Free or Die
in the Granite State** (*continued*)

it's worth it, and I can guarantee you that you'll never feel so relaxed as after a day of riding an Alpine Slide. The scenery at Attitash—the grassy meadows and slopes, the jagged chalky peaks of the White Mountains on the horizon—is amazing. Nearby are North Conway Village (narrow streets lined by art galleries, gem shops, bookstores and family-owned restaurants), the Basin, and the Flume—a seventy-foot waterfall you walk to along a gentle trail that spans glacial gorges via covered bridge. If you want romance, pack strawberries, chocolate, and wine and hike to the Flume after dinner.

3. Have Tea at Kimball Castle
   (www.kimballcastle.com)

Cost: Free. Location: Belknap Point, Gilford. A little-known fact is that the couple that bought and resides in the historic and majestic Kimball Castle is willing to welcome visitors and give them a tour. They're hoping, eventually, to raise the million dollars needed to renovate the castle and turn it into a hotel. For now, the castle is still beautiful. It is made from English oak and huge blocks of red granite. In 1895 Benjamin Ames Kimball, a local railroad baron, hired a hundred Italian stonemasons to build it. He modeled it on a fortress he saw in Germany on the Rhine. His fortress sits on a high point above Lake Winnipesaukee and has 300-degree views of the Broads. Its grounds, twenty acres of gardens landscaped into hills, are bordered by tall stone walls. Adjacent is a nature preserve

66 In 1895 Benjamin Ames Kimball, a local railroad baron, hired a hundred Italian stonemasons to build [his castle]. He modeled it on a fortress he saw in Germany on the Rhine. 99

with 260 acres of hiking and cross-country skiing trails.

4. Hail the Old Man of the Mountain
   (www.visitwhitemountains.com)

Cost: free. Location: I-93, Franconia Notch State Park. The Old Man of the Mountain was a dignified, big-nosed old man, a natural granite sculpture looking out, seventy feet up, from a grand ridge. He has been immortalized by Daniel Webster, Nathaniel Hawthorne, and the Granite State's seal. Several years ago, his nose fell off. Since then he is not the same. But one can still visit Franconia Notch Park, where he lives; hail his face; walk around the Basin (http://www.coping.org/travels/leaf/oldman/narrat.htm), an ancient, glacially carved, thirty-foot-wide granite bowl dubbed the Old Man's foot bath; or hike the trails of the park. Many of the trails are gentle enough for families with small children. Others, like Franconia Notch itself, are two—to three-hour climbs but fine for any novice with sneakers, a sweatshirt, a sandwich, and a bottle of water in a backpack.

5. Find Gold at Ruggles Mine
   (www.rugglesmine.com)

Cost: $10 for kids (four to eleven), $20 for adults. Location: Grafton. Okay, there's no gold. Originally, Ruggles was a mica mine, and mica's everywhere. The trails glint with it. Amethyst, garnet, rose and smoky quartz, topaz, and more dot the caves and walls of ▶

the canyons. The mine's owners say that of
the 150 mineral types buried in the rocks,
it's the uranium ones, such as gummite and
autunite, that collectors prize most. The $20
entry seems steep, but you can enter with a
bucket and keep what you find. And really,
it's exploring the long, winding tunnels,
whispering in the huge dark caves, and
crawling around in the bright white quarry
that I'd pay for. When I was a kid my parents
took me and my sister here, and we both
remember it. The mine sits atop Isinglass
Mountain where the air is crisp and you
can enjoy views of nearby ranges.

6. Go Tubing on Lake Winnipesaukee
   (www.anchormarine.net)

Cost: $30 a day for rental (waterskiing
or tubing package). Because Lake
Winnipesaukee is so deep, long, and
clean, it's perfect for water sports. More
than two hundred forested islands dot the
lake, and navigating them is an adventure.
One can water-ski and tube in the Broads, a
mile-long open stretch at the lake's center,
or anchor off an island and swim. Or explore,
heading to any of the area hotspots, like
Meredith Bay (Frankensundae, a great
make-your-own-sundae place, has a lakeside
patio and its own docks), Wolfeboro (the
downtown contains galleries, shops with
local artisans' wares, restaurants), or the
Weirs. Try threading Sally's Gut—the
trickiest channel on the lake—or cruising
by the Witches, a cluster of glacial rocks
that poke out of a shady pass and resemble

66 Because Lake
Winnipesaukee
is so deep, long,
and clean, it's
perfect for water
sports. More than
two hundred
forested islands
dot the lake, and
navigating them is
an adventure. 99

witches' heads. Good lake maps have dive sites marked—with a wetsuit, a diver can check out the sunken steamboats from the early 1900s, the dozens of capsized and abandoned cruisers, or the deserted underwater Naval marine laboratory. Around five o'clock, loons call across the waters, particularly near the nature sanctuaries, but really, across the whole lake. Most marinas rent boats: speedboats, windsurfers, Sunfishes, etc. I've included a sample: Anchor Marine in Weirs Beach, where a twenty-foot Sea Ray Sport (seats seven, 135 horsepower) goes for $120 (two hours), $210 (four hours), or $280 (all day).

7. Bet on the Dogs at the Tracks (www.thelodgeatbelmont.com)

Cost: Your bet. Location: Route 106, Belmont. There are four greyhound tracks in New Hampshire; The Lodge at Belmont is the track of the Lakes Region. Compared to the Speedway, in nearby Loudon, where NASCAR Nextel Cup events are held in late June and mid-September, the dog tracks are cozy and down-home. At the dog tracks, there are dogs, locals, young trainers, runners—a whole subculture. When I was a kid, my friends worked here, and said it was the best job they ever had. Is it cruel to race dogs? Probably. Nevertheless, in New Hampshire, going to the tracks seems like a fun thing to do. There's an on-site lodge, with a Cajun-themed restaurant that local businessmen love and use for dinner meetings. The track sponsors a program ▶

for those who wish to adopt a greyhound (www.gpa-cnhc.org).

8. Take a Cruise on the *Mount* (www.cruisenh.com)

Cost: For a jazz and champagne brunch cruise, $39 for adults and $18 for kids; for a day cruise, $22 for adult and $10 for kids. Built in 1888 from the hull of a vessel destroyed in a fire that also destroyed most of the Weirs, the MS *Mount Washington* is Lake Winnipesaukee's oldest and grandest cruise ship. It is 230 feet long, white, multi-decked, formerly a steamship, and it contains several restaurants, dance halls, and lounges. During summer and through fall it offers narrated day cruises around the lake, as well as dinner/dance cruises. The buffet includes fresh lobster, and live bands play. In October the ship has foliage-viewing specials: $99 for two adults and two kids (includes dinner and entertainment). The *Mount* is a local icon: all the boaters on the lake wave to it as it passes. Our high school often held proms on it; the ship also does weddings, and its captain officiates.

9. Go Tide-Pooling at Wallace Sands

Cost: Free. Location: Route 1A, Rye. Wallace Sands is a long quiet beach near Portsmouth. Near the stone wall that separates it from the grasses behind, the sand is silty, fine, and white. Toward shore the sand is hard-packed, and children build sand castles during low tide. This beach is where, when we were kids,

66 Built in 1888 . . . the MS *Mount Washington* is Lake Winnipesaukee's oldest and grandest cruise ship. It is 230 feet long, white, multi-decked, formerly a steamship, and it contains several restaurants, dance halls, and lounges. 99

my mother took my sister and me to look for sand dollars and starfish, both of which are abundant. On its right edge, before the shore becomes the private waterfront of Victorian houses, a barnacled stone jetty travels sixty yards into the waves. At the beach's left edge, the shore juts up into cliffs. The sandy path that climbs them is lined by the beach roses (*Rosa rugosa*) that give the air its particular sweet-salty scent. Below the precipice are warm tide pools full of horseshoe crabs and clams. Further left Wallace Sands morphs into another beach, one made entirely of huge boulders that tumble hundreds of feet from cliff to water. This "beach" is always empty but for a few couples who lay blankets and picnic on the rocks. From these rocks (as from the sandy section) one can watch tugboats, barges, and sloops pass by the Isles of Shoals.

At Wallace Sands, the beach house, a large stone edifice, offers fried chicken sandwiches, burgers, and ice cream treats, and contains shockingly pleasant showers. Nearby are great dinner options: my mom's favorite seafood restaurant, Newick's (www.newicks.com), in Dover, began fifty years ago as a roadside stand where fishermen fried and sold extra catch. It sits on Great Bay and has ocean-side patio seating, a gift shop, and live lobsters in tanks, and it serves fabulous stuffed haddock and sole, fried clams, boiled lobster with drawn butter, etc., at low prices. (Kids eat free Sundays.) In Portsmouth's downtown, my mom's other favorite restaurant, the Stockpot, sits on the bay ▶

66 At Wallace Sands, the beach house, a large stone edifice, offers fried chicken sandwiches, burgers, and ice cream treats, and contains shockingly pleasant showers. 99

and offers down-home American dishes, chowders, and pies; it has a cozy dark-wood interior with plate-glass windows from which you can see the three famous antique tugboats that are still helping ships in and out of the harbor. A few blocks away is my mom's favorite French pastry shop, Breaking New Grounds (it used to be called Café Brioche), which makes perfect espresso, cream puffs, and chocolate croissants.

10. Visit the Bunkers at Odiorne Point (www.nhstateparks.com/odiorne.html)

Cost: Weekdays, free; weekends, $3 for adults, free for kids. Location: Route 1A, Rye. Odiorne Point—a former military base, now a state park—is on the New Hampshire coast. When I was a kid, the bunkers were open and one could crawl around inside their sandy interiors. Now the bunkers are filled in. Their tops are (as they were originally) grassy knolls, so they meld somewhat into the landscape. But one can still run up the sporadic humpy hills and call it running up a bunker, as one can still wander the wilderness of Odiorne, which includes acres of rocky oceanfront, a sunken forest of five-thousand-year-old tree stumps pickled by brine, and a wide golden marsh that looks solid because it's covered by cattails. Adjacent to the marsh is a secret hidden sandy beach (where the water is warm, though you'll share it with sand crabs), and, within the acres of brambles, birches, and pines, neglected memorials in clearings and a moss-covered marble bench or two around worn plaques.

There are trails for biking and cross-country skiing; at the point's southern tip, a fifteen-foot-wide jetty that one can run upon stretches a half-mile into the bay. At the park's entrance is a marine museum ($1 entry) with a gift shop and hands-on ocean-life exhibits for children.

After Odiorne, one can drive to Portsmouth for dinner. But my father's favorite follow-up is to tour the USS *Albacore*, a retired naval submarine (http://www.tripadvisor.com/ GetawayDestination-g46209-Portsmouth_ New_Hampshire.html; 600 Market Street, Portsmouth). It's a free museum with exhibits, but most of all, it's a naval submarine that you can walk around in.

11. Skinny-dip at Gilford Beach, After Midnight

Cost: Free. Location: Route 11A, across from Sawyers Dairy Bar, Gilford. The beach is only open to local residents, unless you trespass. To do this, just park a ways away and walk through the thin patch of woods to the shore (avoiding the beach road and gatehouse). The beach is gorgeous and clean, with a floating dock you can swim to and dive from; the snack shack makes great hot dogs and burgers. By late June, the water is nicely warm. I suggest going after midnight, swimming out to the dock, shucking your suit, and diving off. If you want to avoid trespassing, Ellacoya State Park (and beach) is open to all ($5 per car) and very beautiful, long, and quiet (www.nhstateparks.com/ ellacoya.html). ▶

> 66 By late June, the water is nicely warm. I suggest going after midnight, swimming out to the dock, shucking your suit, and diving off. 99

**Thirteen Ways to Live Free or Die
in the Granite State** *(continued)*

12. Rent a Boat and a House on an Island

This costs money. But living in a cottage on
an island for a week is delightful—walking
mornings around the island, swimming in
the evening. The islands of Winnipesaukee
are largely hilly, forested, undeveloped, and
without stores. The weather in summer is
breezy, in the eighties; the water is clear and
cool. For about $1,000 a week, you (and four
friends?) can rent a classic cottage. My
example (www.yankeepedlarrealtors.com/
proddir/prod/110/602) is a beautiful two-
bedroom, one-bath camp (sleeps five) on
Winter Harbor, with a large dock, private
shore, and expansive views of the Ossipee
Mountains; available for $1,350 a week. For
$3,000, you can rent an all-out treat-yourself
mecca: a 4,800-square-feet, seven-bedroom,
four-bath contemporary lakefront house on
Black Cat Island with high ceilings, skylights,
a game room with pool table and big-screen
TV, and outside, a forty-foot deck with
sunken, full-size Jacuzzi. The ad says the house
sleeps twenty. I can't do the math, but if you
went in with a bunch of friends, this might be
affordable (http://www.greatrentals.com/
NH/5005.html). When I was a kid, my parents
took me on tropical vacations: to St. Thomas,
Cancun, Hawaii, etc. They were great, but I
barely remember them. There's something
very particular about Winnipesaukee's secret-
seeming islands. Maybe it's that it is easy to
feel like the lake is yours, or that the lack of
sophisticated nightlife options will force you
to sit around a fire and talk about dorky
things you would never otherwise discuss.

Maybe it's the basic facilities. If the cabin you pick has ugly plaid couches, the pancakes you make will taste all the better.

A free option: island squatting. Rent a boat, a canoe, whatever, and pack a tent and sleeping bag. Many of the undeveloped islands—Rattlesnake or Bear, for example— are hilly, forested, and dotted by vacant camps (with handy barbecue facilities). They have public toilets (though they may be outhouses) and are lined all around by slopey, sandy beaches.

13. Go Tax-Free Shopping

Cost: Cheap. It's cheesy, and it's consumerist. But only in New Hampshire can tax-free outlet shopping be done year round. I suggest the outlet malls in North Conway or Tilton. Prices are incredibly low. Both Tilton (sixty-five-plus stores) and North Conway (Settlers' Green and White Mountain Outlets) have the basics like Banana Republic, J.Crew, Gap, Nine West, Liz Claiborne, Coach, Polo Ralph Lauren, Mikasa . . . North Conway also has Crate and Barrel, Calvin Klein, Ann Taylor, Corning Revere, L.L.Bean. If you shop in North Conway, you can go hiking afterwards, to the Basin, the Flume, etc., to clear your head of worldly thoughts. If you prefer shopping mall-style, try the Mall at Rockingham Park (near Salem, New Hampshire) or Pheasant Lane (near Nashua, New Hampshire). Both are just over the Massachusetts border, and they are each multilevel "super malls" with fountains, palm trees, and relatively high-end stores. ∾

> ❝ If the cabin you pick has ugly plaid couches, the pancakes you make will taste all the better. ❞

Land of *Twenty Grand*
Best Loot, Hikes, Snack Shacks, and Dive Bars

Best Loot

1. Granite

My mom used to drive back roads (like Routes 106 and 107) up into northern New Hampshire, in order to find free granite blocks. Large, rectangular, rough-hewn. She wanted them to serve as front steps and fence posts. She found them along the road, lying by the foundations of abandoned or burnt-out houses, or in people's yards (she asked the owners if she could have them and the owners said sure, or gave them to her for a few bucks). The closer you get to the White Mountains, the more granite blocks you find sitting around.

2. Liquor

Just over the state line, on I-93 North (and visible from the highway), is a large state liquor store that Massachusetts residents often trek to, to buy tax-free alcohol. The prices are low, and most state liquor stores have neon orange signs marking slash-down sales throughout. These state "outlets" are, like Dunkin Donuts, ubiquitous in New Hampshire—in Gilford, my favorite sits next to the cinema, the cash/pawn/gun shop, and the swap-meet. It's an outlet, but it still sells fancy boxed liqueurs and esoteric eighteen-year-old scotches.

> 66 These state [liquor] "outlets" are, like Dunkin Donuts, ubiquitous in New Hampshire—in Gilford, my favorite . . . sells fancy boxed liqueurs and esoteric eighteen-year-old scotches. 99

3. Coins

There are several great coin shops in Concord: Concord Coins, on 5 South State Street; Concord Coins & Memorabilia (has baseball cards and games), 84 South State Street; and the Village Coin Shop, 51 Route 125.

4. Candy

In Concord: The Granite State Candy Shop, 13 Warren Street. The shop has tight quarters, its vats behind the counter; the chocolates are hand-dipped on the premises, and the isles are packed with candies of all kinds (old-fashioned and new). It's run by the grandchildren of the Greek immigrant who opened the store in 1927. If you're in Manchester: visit Van Otis Chocolates (www.vanotis.com). I don't even like fudge, but the Van Otis Swiss fudge is not to be believed. It is not even fudge, really—it's a silk chocolate cloud shaped like a square. It's light, basically—as mascarpone is to regular cheese. You can order it online. Or you can go to the store, which has been in operation since 1935. My mom drives an hour to Manchester just to get the fudge.

5. Antiques

New Hampshire is a great place to go antiquing—because so many houses are old and the residents don't think much of getting rid of antiques cheaply. Antique Alley, on Route 4 between Concord and Portsmouth, has a cluster of shops: five hundred dealers within twenty miles. For something less concentrated, try driving ▶

Route 25 up toward North Conway, or Route 3 toward Meredith; little-known and thus treasure-filled antique stores dot the roads. My favorite pit stop: the Moultonborough Country Store (http://www.nhcountrystore.com/). In operation since 1781, it has many cavernous wooden rooms and sells penny candy, wrought iron and brass hardware, and New England goods like maple syrup, honey, and jams; candles, cookware, weather vanes, slippers, and leather goods. Best, it has an antique, nickel-operated peep-machine, where you can watch nineteenth-century ladies change their clothes.

6. Fresh Produce, Maple Syrup, Honey, and Blueberry Pie

Farm stands are plentiful from Concord on north. Here are some of my favorites in Gilford: Beans & Greens, where my sister worked as a kid, sells baked goods, syrups and jams, fresh produce. They really make the workers toil in the fields, and they bake their own breads and pies. They also sell plants, offer a corn maize (August). and let you pick your own strawberries (June). For fruit: in July, my mom favors high-bush blueberries at Stoneybrook Farm and raspberries at Smith's Farm; in September, apples at Smith's Farm.

Five Best Hikes

1. Belnap Peak, Gilford

Belnap peak is an easy fifty-minute hike, and at the summit is a seventy-foot fire tower. At any time, a ranger is doing a shift in it,

66 In operation since 1781, [the Moultonborough Country Store] has many cavernous wooden rooms and sells penny candy . . . New England goods . . . [and] has an antique, nickel-operated peep-machine, where you can watch nineteenth-century ladies change their clothes. 99

18

usually reading a book in the wooden hut at the top. One can climb the tower (via seven wooden step ladders) and visit the ranger in his hut. From it, you can see all of the Lakes Region. If you bring the ranger a snack, you can also look through many special binoculars. It's pretty stunning. The rounded top of Belknap itself is warm boulder tops, scattered grasses, wildflowers, and clumps of wild blueberries and strawberries. In the woods a few feet off is a pump-your-own spring-water machine, and somehow the water it pumps is sweet and tastes like bread.

2. Mount Chocorua, Route 16, West Ossipee (hikethewhites.com/chocorua.html)

Chocorua (3,500 feet) can be hiked in two to three hours. Its head is warm, rocky, bare, and has views in all directions (www .lazydoginn.com/activities.html). Thoreau called it "stern and rugged." It's one of the most photographed mountains in the United States. Lake Chocorua, at the mountain's base, is crystal clear, good for swimming and canoeing, and surrounded by birches and pines. As a kid I loved this hike because of the legend concerning the mountain's namesake— an Indian chief, involved in a torrid affair with a white family, was chased by white men up the mountain and leapt (after cursing the men) from a rocky ledge to his death.

3. Carter Notch (http://www.outdoors.org/ lodging/huts/huts-carter.cfm)

This is the best hike in the world, because of the great Appalachian Mountain Club huts ▶

> " Thoreau called [Mount Chocorua] 'stern and rugged.' It's one of the most photographed mountains in the United States. "

and rocky glacial field at the top. The field is a flat, sunny twenty acres of white boulders; one can fossil hunt or just climb around in it for hours. The hike to the peak is about three hours; kids can do it (I did it as a kid with my family). The AMC huts sleep six and cost as little as $10 a night. Down a path sits a wide log house, where the ranger lives and which is open to hikers, who can lounge there at night (play chess or drink beer and talk by the fire; cook pancakes in the kitchen in the morning).

4. The Flume, Franconia Notch State Park
   (*see "Ride the Alpine Slide"*)

5. Franconia Notch
   (*see "Hail the Old Man on the Mountain"*)

Note: There are AMC huts atop many of the White Mountain peaks. Most trails can be climbed by novices; stash a sleeping bag, snacks, water, and whatever else you desire in a backpack. Hiking any one of them and sleeping in an AMC hut, in late summer or early fall, is, in my mind, the best experience in the world. You get the warmth of a hut, the ruggedness of camping, it's cheap, you'll bond with the people you're with, and the scenery is so beautiful that you'll never forget it.

Snack Shacks

1. The Tamarac

It's just a roadside shack on the way from the Weirs to Meredith. But if you're heading that way, stop for a burger, lobster roll, or popcorn shrimp. It's a hangout, and it's near FunSpot, the cheesiest place to bowl (candlepin or regular) and spend hours playing video games, arcade-style. When I was a teenager? This was the place to meet boys. The employees wore black-and-white-striped uniforms—very cute.

2. Sawyers Dairy Bar, Gilford

Family-owned for fifty years, adjacent to Gilford Beach, Sawyers makes its own ice cream, serves unparalleled burgers, lobster rolls, fried chicken sandwiches, and is topped by a fifties-style rotating sign.

3. The Lobster Shack, Weirs Beach

A favorite of bikers, families, and couples. It's not fancy, but it serves the best lobster in the Lakes Region.

4. The Ice House, Route 1B, Rye (http://seacoastnh.com/Food/Penny_ Gourmet/The_Ice_House/)

En route to the beaches, known as a New Hampshire "best kept secret," the Ice House is a casual, shack-style restaurant with grassy field and picnic tables outside. Known for its frappes, great for fried seafood, sandwiches, burgers. Perfect pit stop on the way to or from the ocean.

5. Newick's, Dover (www.newicks.com)

On the great bay. Sit on the outside patio and watch the boats in the harbor. Voted ▶

Land of *Twenty Grand* (continued)

New Hampshire's best seafood restaurant, it's down-home, sprawling, and wooden, and serves amazing fare at low prices. Kids eat free on Sundays.

Dive Bars

Any bar in New Hampshire is probably a dive bar. Jeremiah's, in Gilford, though, is probably the only one where you can smoke cigarettes and sing karaoke while watching blonde biker babes dance on a black-and-white-checkered dance floor. If you don't like to karaoke, you can play pool at any one of the four billiard tables (though the twenty-something guys around the tables tend to fart a lot, and you'll be lucky to find chalk).

> Any bar in New Hampshire is probably a dive bar.

Don't miss the next book by your favorite author. Sign up now for AuthorTracker by visiting www.AuthorTracker.com.